Rebirth

The Dance of Cherry Blossoms

AUDREY MURPHY

Copyright © 2022 Audrey Murphy. All rights reserved.

The characters and events portrayed in this book are fictitious. Any similarity to real persons, living or dead, is coincidental and not intended by the author.

No part of this book may be reproduced, or stored in a retrieval system, or transmitted in any form or by any means, electronic, mechanical, photocopying, recording, or otherwise, without express written permission of the author.

My heartfelt thanks goes out to a number of people, who read my book at different stages of its development: To Amber Nicholson, and Stacy and Barb Zika, my first readers, who set me on a path of revision. Special thank-you's to my husband, Mike, and son, Jason, who read Dance of Cherry Blossoms numerous times. Their patience and critical remarks helped me tweak my prose and refine this novel. Thank-you. God has blessed me with a wonderful family. Again, many thanks to all of you for your time and diligence.

Therefore, "they are before the throne of God and serve him day and night in his temple; and he who sits on the throne will shelter them with his presence. 'Never again will they hunger; never again will they thirst. The sun will not beat down on them,' nor any scorching heat. For the Lamb at the center of the throne will be their shepherd; 'he will lead them to springs of living water.' 'And God will wipe away every tear from their eyes.'"

Revelation 7:15-17 (NIV)

Prologue

Saturday, July 29, 2006. Small circles of light had sliced through the darkness from one location to another and had exposed stone, brick, and latticed framework. Glowing LED globe lights had towered above like beacons of hope on the campus of Adelphi. And the sound of footsteps had splashed through puddles of rain as police scoured the university's grounds. And I'd prayed. I'd hoped.

Chapter 1 - Omens
The Morning of Saturday, May 27, 2006

Alex and I had owned our dance studio, The Silver Slipper, in Manhattan for thirty-four years. After my family, it had remained something I'd loved, at least ninety-nine percent of the time. Any job has a one percent spoiler. For me that had involved those few pain-in-the-rear students who hadn't listened or who'd had their own agenda, like looking for a brief romance in our dance classes. And we'd had a few, but one in particular had won the prize for pushing my button.

As usual, our part-time instructors, Nick and Kayla, had covered Saturday dance lessons, and Alex and I had had a two-day weekend together. Weather predictions had forecasted a rainless sunny day. My wife and I had gotten up extra early to get work done at home, then we'd intended to take a leisurely walk in Central Park. Alex had begun vacuuming, and I'd volunteered to clean the bathrooms. Then, I had begun working on the computer.

With earplugs in, I had pulled up the registration site for our dance studio, and I'd scanned enrollment for the next six-week session. *Lower than the last one. What am I going to do? Alex loves The Silver Slipper as much as I do. If enrollment doesn't pick up, we'll have to file bankruptcy. How do I tell her that?*

I'd heard dishes rattling in the kitchen. *She's started making breakfast. Better hurry and get finished.* My fingers had struck the keyboard faster. And as if in tempo, a light tapping had danced across my back from shoulder to shoulder. My fingers had frozen on the keys, and our dance studio's financial situation had vanished from my mind. The rhythmic patter, light as a whisper, had felt like the pad of a finger tapping out a coded message. A split second later, a pull, like a magnetic force, had accompanied it. *An omen? No. I don't believe in premonitions.* But a memory from my youth had revisited me. *What about that dream I had in Greenstone, Missouri? I dreamt the awning on Pop Bradshaw's soda fountain shop was falling. His health deteriorated, and the man who had treated me like a son died.* My gaze had rerouted from the screen, had darted to the collage of family photos that had hung on the wall in front of my desk. My dark-haired beauty and me on our wedding day. Our married offspring. Grandkids. Our families in Missouri. Like a weather prediction had broadcast a vicious storm, threatening to seize one of them, like a warning that a piece of my heart would soon blow away, I'd understood. *One of my loved ones is in danger.*

The rhythmic tap, tap, tap had changed, and as if needles had borne deep into my skin, I'd flinched. A foul taste had snaked its way up my throat, and I had forced it back down. And my stomach had done a series of somersaults. *God help me. Who is it? And what's going to happen?* I'd studied the family photos, then had searched the computer screen for His answer. But all I'd seen were students' names I had registered for dance lessons.

My wife's call of, "Ty, breakfast is ready," had carried to my office area, a nook in our living room with a chair and desk. *Caffeine. That's what I need.*

Still in her pajamas and wearing no makeup, Alex had looked beautiful as she'd worked in the kitchen. She'd flipped the last pancake onto a plate and had smiled in that special way of hers. Under different circumstances she would've aroused me and made me lose my train of thought. But certain something sinister had lain in wait for someone I loved, my stomach's gyrating acrobatics had continued.

I'd kissed her full lips and had attempted to mask the physical warfare going on inside me. She had put the coffeepot and cups on the table. I'd poured our coffee and added sugar and cream to Alex's. "Hope you're hungry, Ty."

I had no appetite, but I'd forced a smile. "Just black coffee for me this morning." However, she'd placed two plates with mountains of caramel-brown pancakes, topped with fresh strawberries and whip cream on the table. And Alex had sat across from me. The cream had melted, and red rivulets had flowed down the pancakes.

I'd downed the coffee and poured myself another cup before I had cut my pancakes into bite-size portions. But when I'd gotten the first speared piece to my mouth, my stomach had churned. I'd placed the fork on my plate and picked up *The New York Times* from the kitchen table. I'd emptied my second cup of coffee as I had read.

"Ty, better eat those before–"

"Listen to this." My diversion had redirected her attention. "A robber attacked some woman after she exited a train yesterday.

Punched her in the stomach and took off with her purse. You laugh when I tell you I don't want you riding the subway by yourself. And our daughters . . . well, I get that oh no, not again look when I tell them to pay attention to their surroundings. Just because I want to keep all of you safe."

"Bad things can happen anywhere. In a grocery store. A hair salon. You can't protect me and the girls every minute of every day. But I love you for wanting to."

"Please, be aware of what's happening around you. That's all I'm asking."

"Okay. And you stop being a worrywart."

As far as her excursions alone, she, like our daughters, had thought I blew hot air when I warned them about the dangers of the city. I'd speared a forkful of soggy pancakes but, having no appetite, swallowed it in one gulp. "Delicious." The same sickening taste I'd had sitting at the computer had inched up my throat. But I'd made a silent vow. *No way am I telling her about that. I'll sound ridiculous.* I'd gotten up to scrape the rest of my pancakes into the garbage disposal.

The phone on the wall had rung, and as I'd reached for it, I dropped the plate, and it had broken into pieces. Alex had gotten up from the table and begun to clean up the mess I'd made. And I'd observed that one long, tapered piece she'd picked up looked like the blade of a knife. *Another omen?* With the phone pressed to my ear, my eyes had darted to the clock on the wall. *Who'd call this early? What's happened?*

"Ty." A sob, pitiful and weak, had squeaked through the receiver, and though uncharacteristic of his masculine voice, I'd identified the caller as my deceased sister's husband.

I had hung up and relayed the bad news to my wife. "That was Drew. He and Jenny are on their way to Barnes-Jewish. Brad's fine, but his wife, Hannah, sustained injuries from a car accident, and she's been airlifted to the hospital's trauma center."

Alex's hand had shot to her mouth, and I'd deciphered the alarm etched into her warm, brown eyes. "Pack a few clothes and toiletries for us, Honey. I'll call our kids and tell them Hannah's in the hospital, and that we're taking the first flight we can get to Saint Louis."

Chapter 2 - Hannah
Saturday Afternoon

From Lambert Saint Louis International Airport, we'd taken a taxi to the Washington University Medical Campus. Our driver had dropped us at the Charles F. Knight Building.

We'd wheeled our small carry-on baggage into the level one trauma center and had stopped at the desk for information. Alex had called Robert. She'd asked him to inform his two sisters about their cousins' hospitalization. And that's when it hit me. *I didn't grab the class lists with our students' names and phone numbers. I need to cancel the classes Alex and I teach. Our two instructors handle their classes just fine. But if they split-up to cover ours that won't work, and I don't want our students to get annoyed. With our low enrollment, we can't afford to have students quit.*

"Honey," I'd interrupted Alex from her conversation, "ask Robert if he can get our class lists out of the desk at The Silver Slipper and cancel our Monday through Thursday lessons. We should get back to handle Friday's. Kayla and Nick have a key to The Silver Slipper. Have Robert tell them to continue teaching their classes."

Alex had reiterated my request to our son. She'd nodded, affirming he would.

I had called Drew on my cell phone. "On our way up." He'd met us at the elevator as we'd stepped out. An olfactory overload of disinfectants had hit me. I'd identified a heavy bleach smell, amongst a mix of other cleaning solutions. The inset ceiling lights had given off a white glow, and the unblemished white walls and floor, had given the hallway a sterile look. *Hannah's in a clean hospital.*

After Alex had gotten a bear-hug from my former brother-in-law, he had shaken my hand. "How'd you get here so quick?" he'd asked, guiding us to the critical care waiting room.

"Got lucky," I'd said. Drew's haggard, lined face had sent me a message. "Delta had two seats for a 10:15 departure. How's everyone holding up?"

Silence had set in. He'd wiped a runaway tear rolling down his cheek. "Jenny's knees buckled when she got Brad's call this morning. I caught her. But the God's truth is, I thought I was going down with her. And now all we're doing is waiting and praying our granddaughter's gonna be alright."

Drew had stopped at the doorway, faced us, and cleared his throat. "Better bring you up to speed before we go in. Brad's in no shape to do it. An X-ray showed Hannah's middle rib is broken. That'll heal on its own. But a CT scan showed a perforation in her left lung. The other driver pulled out from a side road, and Hannah got the brunt of the impact."

She's petite, like my sister, Allison, was. The air bag's force, even the seatbelt's constriction, could have caused the puncture.

"Brad said they'd taken Hannah to be prepped for surgery about twenty minutes before Jenny and I arrived. But the bottom line is we haven't gotten any news yet. How long can it take to suture a perforation?"

I'd had no inkling, and I'd just shook my head. "Who's her surgeon?"

"A Dr. Hartmann," Drew had said. "But not even Brad got to meet him. After Hannah's X-ray, they rushed her to surgery."

The broken piece of plate, shaped like the blade of a knife, the rivulets of red whipped cream. The omens warned me about my niece's surgery. But I can't tell Drew. He'd never believe me.

"If something should happen to her, I don't know what I'd do," Drew had said. "And Jenny, she's torn up with worry. She won't cry in front of Brad, but she took a walk, said she needed to stretch her legs. But she returned with red eyes."

"Except for whiplash, Brad's fine physically. Emotionally, he's a mess. He's clammed up, scared out of his wits. And I get that."

Drew had gotten it. He'd mourned the loss of his first wife, my sister. I'd sent Allison a silent plea. *You're with the Guy upstairs. Put in a word for your daughter.*

Chapter 3 - Desperation
Late Afternoon

People with bloodshot eyes and red noses had occupied the critical care waiting room. And others with their eyes closed and heads hung had left me no doubt they'd sat for a lengthy period of time.

As we'd approached, Brad's varnished eyes had held steady on his wedding band, and he'd turned it around and around on his finger. His pale, fatigued face and hunched shoulders had displayed defeat. And the red border around Jenny's eyes had confirmed she'd been crying, but she'd forced a weak smile.

"I'm so sorry this happened," Alex had said. Her wet, brown eyes had articulated compassion.

Brad hadn't acknowledged her. He'd continued turning his thin, gold wedding band around and around. Without looking up, and with one downward stroke, his fist had struck the table, as if he'd had a burst of adrenaline. "It's my fault. I didn't react fast enough."

Alex had flinched. I'd pulled out a chair for her, and her tall, slender body had lowered onto it, as if it had been a spike. Brad's glazed eyes had refocused on his wedding band. His body had folded into itself, and his drooped shoulders and downcast eyes had fixated on his shoes. He had looked burdened with guilt.

I'd sat next to him. "The accident wasn't your fault." Hannah's husband hadn't acknowledged my words. He'd folded his hands in his lap and closed his eyes.

My wife had opened her small suitcase. She'd taken out the book she'd started reading on the plane, and she'd sat in the chair to my right. The sheen of Alex's dark hair, the warmth of her brown eyes, her fair complexion, and full lips had spoken to me. But besides her beauty, something else had caused me to fall in love with her, too. Her kindness. Brad's predicament had tugged at my heart, too. And a question had probed my mind. *What if my niece, his wife dies? Poor Brad. I can't imagine how he'll handle it.*

Jenny had busied herself by working on a crossword puzzle, and Drew had closed his eyes. *He's* pretending *to sleep, but I bet he's praying.* In an attempt to occupy my mind, I had eavesdropped on other peoples' conversations. But after a while, their dialogues had turned into a buzz of racket, and my sense of responsibility had awakened my conscience. *Should've called Mom and Dad. No. Call after Hannah gets out of surgery,* I'd reasoned. *If her lung repair goes well, I'll have good news to counteract the bad. Neither of them is in the best of health.*

The receptionist had led four doctors to families in the critical care waiting room. In a subtle manner, I'd glanced at my watch. *Something's wrong. Hannah's doctor should have spoken with us by now.*

Brad had cupped his hands over his wet eyes, and his body had shaken in unison with his ragged sobs. *He's reached his breaking point.* I'd reached over and patted him on the back, and I had noticed a guy in blue scrubs with a linebacker's physique had approached the receptionist. *He's a doctor?* The receptionist had come out of the enclosed cubicle and led him to our table. "Dr. Hartmann, this is Mr. Brown," she'd pointed at Brad. "And these are other members of Hannah's family." Brad had stood and stuck out his hand, and the receptionist had left us.

I'd scrutinized the doctor. *No older than forty-five. Bald on top, like me. But he has no hair on the sides, either.*

"Your wife's out of recovery and in a room. A broken rib punctured her left lung and excess air got into the membrane around her lungs. That caused pressure and wouldn't allow the lungs to expand. I've inserted a chest tube to drain the excess air. In two days, Hannah's chest should inflate properly, and I'll release her. Today, one visitor at a time. She needs to rest. Any questions?"

"Inserting a tube took that long?" Brad had said.

"No. But monitoring Hannah after surgery took longer than usual. As a rule, a patient's vitals are back to normal in two hours. But your wife had anxiety, and it took longer to get her blood pressure down. She had to remain in the Post Anesthetic Care Unit until it was within normal range."

Not only had I'd taken in every word Dr. Hartmann had said, I'd examined him further. *No eyebrows? And his face is as smooth as a baby's butt. His forearms are hairless, too. Bad case of alopecia.*

The tension in Brad's face had relaxed. "Thank-you, doctor. Didn't mean to get sharp with you. Nerves."

Dr. Hartmann had cleared his throat. "I understand. Now, there's something else I need to discuss with you. Hannah's CT had also shown a suspicious mass. You and your family had a lot to deal with at the time, so I decided to exam it during the repair and get a biopsy before I spoke to you about it. It's possible it's an abscess, so I started Hannah on an antibiotic. But the mass could also be a sign of underlying endobronchial lung cancer. I'll have the lab report within two days."

Brad 's eyes had taken on a wet glaze, and his face had turned white.

"Oh, Lord," Jenny had said. She'd leaned against Drew, as if she'd needed support.

A runaway tear had rolled down Alex's cheek, and I'd choked back my own emotion.

"Does your wife smoke?" Dr. Hartmann had asked.

"No. In fact, she's tried to get me to give up cigarettes. Thinks it's a bad habit. But I can't kick it; I've smoked a pack a day since age seventeen."

"Did you smoke indoors?"

Drew's complexion had turned red. "No. Outside. Always."

"Good," the doctor had nodded. "Has she complained about shortness of breath? Coughed up blood? Run a fever? Lost weight?"

"No. None of that."

Alex had removed a tissue from her purse, blotted her cheeks, then taken hold of my hand. We'd had a business to run, and we hadn't visited our Missouri relatives often enough, but like me, she'd understood the bond of family. Alex and I had talked about how we dreaded the time when our parents would die. But the possibility of my young niece dying from cancer had struck me as unjust and cruel. *She'll miss out on raising her daughter, like my sister, Allison, missed sharing her motherly love with Hannah*, had shot through my mind.

Dr. Hartmann had redirected his attention back to Brad. "Your wife panicked when I told her about the biopsy. About the possibility she might have lung cancer. She'll want to discuss that possibility with you, Mr. Brown. Please remain optimistic."

Brad had spent more than an hour in his wife's room. The rest of us had remained in the waiting room, antsy to get a peek at Hannah.

Jenny and Drew had gotten a few brief minutes with her, and Alex and I had gone in last. Asleep and peaceful, my niece's eyelids had served as canopies, but I'd known her eyes; they had the same trusting expression as those of her deceased mother's. Her long, brown hair, small features, and slight build had resembled Allison's, too. And I had imagined that if she would have smiled, her lips would've parted with the corners turned up, the delicate, shy way my younger sibling's had.

Drew had returned to sit with his wife, and Alex and I had joined the others in the waiting room. I'd had unfinished business to deal with. *Dad's still able to run the soda fountain shop in Greenstone, Missouri,* I'd reasoned. *But what if he gets worked up and has another stroke? And I'm sure Mom will break down and cry. I don't want to upset them. Hannah is the only part of Allison they have left.* Words had circled around and around in my head as I had tried to organize what I'd had to say to them. *A car accident punctured Hannah's lung, but it's been repaired.* Then I'd hit the roadblock. *How do I tell them she might have cancer?*

"Hello, Partridge residence," her cheerful voice had sounded melodic.

"Hi Mom."

"Hello, Son. It's good to hear your voice."

I'd told her about the car accident, about Hannah's repaired lung, and she'd gasped. But when I'd mentioned the C word, a high-pitched scream had drilled into my ear. That's when my dad had taken charge of the phone. "Ty, what's wrong?"

I had filled him in, grateful he hadn't gone to pieces like my mom had.

"We'll leave right away."

"It's best if you and Mom stay home. Brad, Drew, Jenny, Alex, and I are with her. The doctor wants Hannah to rest. She's sleeping now, and we're sitting in the waiting room. I'll keep you posted. Alex and I will take a taxi to your house. Tomorrow we'll all go together to visit her."

"Okay. You know best, Son."

I'd heard my mother sobbing in the background. "I love you guys. Tell Mom for me?"

"Sure will. We'll have a pot of stew waiting for you. And we'll have Allison's bedroom ready."

I don't want to sleep in my deceased sister's room.

The cab driver had pulled into my parents' gravel driveway. Groupings of gray clouds had peppered the firmament with blemishes, and far-off, beyond my folks' house, a backdrop of red lightning had slashed through the sky. The hair on my arms had stood in attention. Another omen?

Chapter 4 - Visitors
Saturday Night

Mom had led Alex to my sister's room, but I had wanted to get a peek at my childhood bedroom. And I'd gotten a surprise. *What's up with all those boxes stacked on top of the bed? It looks like a catchall for storage.*

I'd walked down the hall and stood at the doorway of Allison's former room. My mom had Allison's quilt pulled down. "It's firm, Alex. I think you'll sleep better here."

I won't. "Mom," I had interrupted, "what's in those boxes on top of my old bed?"

Just clothes Dad and I want to get rid of."

They never parted with that many boxes of clothes when I lived here. I'll clear the bed, and Alex and I will sleep in my old room. But I hadn't gotten the opportunity to voice my preference. Mom had asked if we'd mind my sister's room, and Alex had spoken up, "Sure Marta. That'll be fine."

Great.

The two of them had continued gabbing in my sister's former bedroom, but I'd gone back to examine the sealed boxes. *There's an A or T marked on the side of them. Memorabilia from Allison's and my childhood? Why'd Mom lie?* I had pulled the tape off of a box marked with T. I'd reached in and taken an item wrapped in newspaper out. As I'd unwrapped it, my memory had peddled back to my fifth Christmas.

It's my favorite toy, Looky Fire Truck. The chipped, red paint had battle scars. And I'd remembered when the missing right wheel had fallen off.

The happy face on the front had eyes that rolled when I'd pulled it, and two firemen bobbed up-and-down. And I had remembered how the bell rung, how I'd giggle. But from that place of childhood memories echoed Dad's voice. "A shovel and coal bucket would have been better, Marta."

I'd found a box with an A marked on it. *Allison can't revisit her childhood treasures*, I'd reasoned. So I had unwrapped it. Her Troll Doll with pink hair and bulging eyes had smiled back at me. *She liked that goofy thing*, I'd reminisced. Inside another balled up wad of newspaper I'd found a Cootie. I'd picked it up and had held it in the palm of my hand. *We assembled those plastic insects together.*

My hungry hands had grabbed for another piece of my sister's life. Barbie in a black-and-white stripe swimsuit had come into view. And I'd remembered my sister saying, "I wish I looked like that." *You were prettier*, my mind had whispered. Then I'd dug down deeper into the box and unwrapped her Betsy McCall. The doll's eyes had stared back at me. A lump had formed in my throat. And I'd looked away. The bond Allison had had with that doll had gotten me choked up. *My sister had needed me, and I left her.*

I hadn't needed to look inside any more boxes. *Memories Mom holds close to her heart*, my inner voice had spoken. *I understand her getting rid of my old toys. But Allison's?* And like fog had dissipated, an answer had come to me. *I guess Mom doesn't need crutches anymore. She has Hannah, the spitting image of my sister. God, please. If Hannah has cancer, make it go away.*

Alex's head had hit the pillow, and she'd fallen asleep. But my mind hadn't unwound, and heartburn had attacked my stomach. The silence had talked to me and turned gears in my brain. It had spun out things I hadn't wanted to think about.

I can't sleep in Allison's bed. The heirloom passed down from Grandma Morgan to my sister had brought back too many childhood memories. Careful to not wake Alex, I'd removed the upper portion of the patchwork quilt Mom had made Allison for her thirteenth birthday. In the dark of night, a clear picture of my deceased sister's pink curtains had held my mind hostage, also.

Heartburn had attacked, and I'd have sworn a blazing fire had scorched my chest. In an attempt to push my memories and concerns aside, I'd blame Mom's stew for my indigestion.

Change position. That'll help. From my back, I'd rolled onto my right side. But it hadn't eased my physical or mental discomforts. *I can't unwind. Think about something else.* But the C word had followed me into my sister's childhood bedroom. *What if Hannah, has cancer?*

To rid my brain of morbid thoughts, I'd decided to start at one hundred and count backward in my head. I'd gotten to number eighty-two, and that's when it had happened, the sensation that a bony finger had poked me in the small of my back. I had flinched and rolled over onto my left side. A man had stood next to the bed, and light had filtered through him. *Am I dreaming?* I'd pushed myself up to a sitting position, and Alex had sighed. The man's lips had formed a broad smile.

Speechless, I'd stared at him. His eyes had twinkled, and a rippling wave had coursed through his chest, as if he'd laughed. And like two blue oceans, whose depth couldn't be measured, those eyes had drawn me in and had held my attention. *Those azure eyes. I've crossed paths with him before. Who is this ghost spared the ravages of death?*

Alex, sound asleep again, had remained curled up on her right side, oblivious to the glowing man's presence. And I'd rationalized, *This is an optical illusion.* But I had closed my eyes and reopened them. *He's still here.* That's when my eyes had taken in all of him. Thin and dressed in a white, long-sleeve shirt and black trousers, he had put his glowing hand up to his white goatee, and as if it had itched, he'd scratched it.

"Think. You know me," he'd said.

His lips didn't part. *It's as if his words are echoing inside my head. How'd he do that? Did he speak through those blue eyes?*

"Congratulations, Ty. You've worked hard to obtain your dancing career. Are you happy, now?"

Taken aback, I hadn't responded.

"Allison loved you when you were kids," he continued, "and she loves you now. Stop beating yourself up. She chose the life she wanted."

The spirit's knowledge had frightened and comforted me at the same time. *He's from the heavenly world. But the cadence of his speech, the tone of his voice. Those eyes. I've met him before, in his human form.*

"Ty," he'd said, his blue eyes, providing him voice. "Yes. You know me."

As I'd pursued the spirit's identity, my heart had pounded like that of a racehorse attempting to get to the finish line. And then I had it. I'd connected the dots. *Those blue eyes, that white handlebar mustache.* "You're Reverend Maynard from Greenstone's church."

"Yes," his voice had echoed inside my head. "The Lord called me home at the ripe old age of ninety-five. I don't possess powers like angels, mind you, but God sent me to help your niece, Hannah. And you, too."

"Why didn't Allison's spirit come?"

"Don't challenge God's authority. He assigned me this task. Like He used me in my human form years ago." The glow emitted through the reverend's body had dimmed, as if he'd experienced a power shortage, and he'd bowed his head. "I'm sorry. Please forgive my show of pride, Lord."

The glow had returned to the spirit's body, and he'd made eye contact with me. "God wants to give you a gift. Keep your eyes fixed on mine."

The reverend's pupils had changed into two deep, dark tunnels. And then, a bright, white light no bigger than the head of a pin had appeared in the center of the right tunnel.

"Hold your eyes steady on the white light," he'd said.

The light had grown in intensity. And without any physical connection, what had felt like small fingers had brushed across my left cheek, and a light floral fragrance had swum up my nose. "Allison?"

"Yes, it's me, Bird. Listen to the reverend. God sent him to help Hannah."

My sister's voice had echoed inside my head, like Reverend Maynard's had. And hearing her use my childhood nickname had warmed my heart. The source of her voice, I was certain, had also come from the white light in the reverend's right pupil. Exhilaration had shot through me. But in the next moment, I'd had second thoughts. *This isn't happening. This is all a dream.* Allison's voice had charged through the white pinpoint of the reverend's eyes, her tone had sharpened, and her volume had grown louder: "You know my voice!"

The white light had grown dimmer.

"Don't go. Please!" I'd cried out.

"Do what Reverend Maynard asks of you," she'd uttered, her voice tainted with stress. "Be a good, big brother, Bird; I need your help. My daughter needs a miracle. She has cancer."

"I won't let you down this time. I promise. "A light touch had brushed across both of my cheeks. My sister's delicate fingers had wiped my tears away. And then Allison had vanished.

Chapter 5 - Spirits?
Sunday Morning, May 28

Alex had had her back to me. Her exhales, little downy puffs, had drifted at marked intervals. The lack of noise from Mom's pots and pans had told me she hadn't gotten up to start breakfast. And since I hadn't heard any movement, I'd presumed Dad had slept in, too. I'd had a restless night. But with the curtain of darkness gone, my mind had circled back to reality. And after I had replayed the night's events over and over in my head, I'd ended up with the same common-sense conclusion: What a whopper of a dream. I'd gotten out of bed quietly and hadn't awoken my wife.

I had made my way to the bathroom, turned on the shower, and chilly water had beaten down on my back. The old pipes had knocked and clanked, like they had when I and Allison, had lived with Mom, and Dad. And my mind had peddled back even further to when Grandma Morgan had owned the house, and we'd visited her. How, as a kid, I'd heard those pipes bang, and I'd thought Grandpa Morgan's spirit had attempted to send me a message. With that remembrance, my dream had skipped through my mind, like a thrown stone across water, and I had chuckled. *Spirits. Yeah, right.*

We'd finished eating the biscuits, pork sausage, and milk gravy Mom had made. All of us had headed for the door to leave for the hospital, and Alex's cell phone had rung. "Hi, Andrea," she answered.

It hadn't mattered that our children were married adults. My wife had remained their go-to person when it came to them checking in. With her ear pressed to her cell phone, she'd gotten in my dad's truck, and I'd followed her to the back seat. Mom and Dad had gotten in, and Charles Partridge had put his foot to the pedal. *Wish I had offered to drive.*

"Hannah's left lung is repaired, but the tube remains in until the excess air in it drains out," Alex had said. "But there's another concern. The surgeon found a mass on one of her lungs. Might be cancer."

My wife had stopped talking, and she'd listened, her ear glued to the phone. "It'll be a couple of days before the lab report is ready. I'll let you know." Another gap of silence had occurred. "Sure, I'll tell her. Hey, how's the case coming along?"

Alex's pursed lips and wrinkled brow were fretful. "You'll do fine. Don't let it get under your skin, and don't forget you have a family. Tom and the kids deserve your attention, too."

I'd waited and waited for their conversation to come to an end. I had wanted to find out what Andrea had said. But my wife's ear had remained pressed against the phone, her exhales saddled with weight. My restriction to one side of the conversation hadn't hindered my ability to draw a conclusion, though. *Our daughter's dealing with a tough case.*

"Okay, Andrea, love you, too. Bye." Alex had turned to me. "She and the case investigator decided the evidence is overwhelming. The driver had slurred speech and wouldn't take a breathalyzer."

"Good. Sounds like a slam dunk," I'd said.

"Andrea doesn't think so."

"Why?"

"Politics."

We'd taken the elevator to the second floor and made our way to the waiting room. Drew and Jenny had greeted us with hugs. But Mom's eyes had filled with tears. Brad had remained seated, his head bowed, his eyes fixated on his wedding ring.

"Been here all night?" Dad had said to Drew and Jenny, though the answer had been obvious. Mom had taken a tissue out of her purse and wiped at her eyes. I had hoped she wouldn't go into a full-blown bawl.

Bulging, craggy bags beneath my fellow high school buddy's eyes had spoken to me, and strands of flyaway, gray hair had protruded from Jenny's ponytail and served as evidence she'd had a restless, worrisome night, too. And both their faces, road maps lined with anxiety, had served as statements of fear for their granddaughter's well-being.

"Yeah," Drew had said. "Wouldn't have slept at home, anyway." Then he'd turned to Jenny, seated next to him. "I need to stretch my legs. Stay and visit. " He'd kissed his wife on the cheek and whispered something in her ear.

"Take a walk with me, Ty."

Alex's eyes had communicated her curiosity, and Mom and Dad had thrown me an inquisitive glance as well.

"Sure," I had said. *Wonder what's up?*

"I'm glad Jenny and I stayed last night," Drew had said. "A little after eleven p.m., Brad came out to the waiting room. He told me he'd gotten groggy and about dozed off in the chair next to Hannah's bed. But he heard her say, 'Mom, I see you in that old man's eyes,' and he perked up. Brad swears Hannah had her head turned to the side, and her eyes were open. But he didn't see Allison, or any man. He told Hannah the sleeping pill caused her to hallucinate. But she cried and insisted she hadn't taken it. What do you think?"

In my keyed-up state, my heart had hammered against my chest, but I'd done my best to look composed. "Yeah, I think he's right about the sleeping pill. But poor Hannah. The wreck, the surgery, that's a lot for her to deal with. I believe stress has thrown Brad for a loop, too."

"Yeah. He stammered when he told me about Hannah."

Drew hadn't bought the possibility that his deceased wife, Allison, my sister, had conversed with their daughter. Why would he? But my sister and Reverend Maynard had spoken to me, too. And though I'd understood what Hannah had experienced had been real, I had had to hold my tongue. *I need to speak to my niece alone.*

The tapping, needlelike jabs while I'd sat at my home computer had flitted through my mind. *This is what the omens attempted to warn me about.*

Drew's eyes had drilled into mine. *He's waiting for me to answer.*

"You know, Brad's right; Hannah's under a lot of stress," I'd said. "A sleeping pill can do funny things to a person. He hit the bull's-eye. That pill messed with her head, and she had a hummer of a hallucination."

Drew's eyes had softened. "Yeah, makes sense." But in the next second, his eyes had displayed anger. "Brad better make sure they don't give my granddaughter anymore of those sleeping pills, or I'll step in and give that Dr. Hartmann a piece of my mind."

Drew and I had reclaimed our seats in the urgent care waiting room. Alex had held a magazine with Angelina Jolie featured on the cover. Jenny had busied herself by working on a crossword puzzle.

And my former brother-in-law had sat next to his wife, stretched out his legs, and closed his eyes. Minutes later, his body had twitched, and he'd surrendered to much needed sleep.

My niece's 'hallucination' had hung in my mind and hadn't allowed me to relax. *Gotta find a way to talk to her alone.*

Slouched in his chair, Brad's downcast eyes had stared at the floor. It looked as if, any moment, he'd have tumbled onto the tile in the waiting area. I'd touched his shoulder, and his body had jolted upright.

"Didn't mean to startle you."

"You didn't."

"Stretch your legs," I'd said. "Take everyone with you to the cafeteria. Get a decent cup of coffee and something to eat. I'll stay with Hannah. Living in New York, I don't see her much. Let me do this small thing."

Brad had released a deep exhale. "Okay. Thanks. I won't be gone long."

Alex had hung back. "Honey, you need another hit of caffeine," I had said. "Better bring me a coffee back, too."

She'd smiled. "Okay."

"Thanks."

I'd sat in the chair next to Hannah's hospital bed, and an inexplicable, faint, floral smell had teased my nose. My gentle touch to her arm had awoken her, and the corners of her lips had turned up. *Just like Allison's shy smile.* "Hi, how are you doing?" I'd spoken softly.

"Uncle Ty. I need to go home. My little girl needs me."

She hadn't answered my question, but I'd understood. Our children are more important than our own life. "You'll be home with Rachel in no time."

"Not if I have cancer."

I'd wanted to reassure her that she didn't, though my sister's spirit had said she did. "You're young. There's no genetic predisposition."

Her eyes had filled with tears, and she'd sobbed. She'd held her trembling hands out to me, like a plea for help, and I had enveloped them in mine. "Yeah, cancer's bad, but that's not all I'm worried about, Uncle Ty."

"What else, then?"

Hannah had masked her face with her hands, and ragged gasps had escaped. Like two dams had burst, currents of tears had broken through and had run down her cheeks. Her body had shaken, and fear had tugged at my heartstrings. I'd removed her hands and enveloped them in mine. "What's wrong," I had said.

"An old man, with a white goatee . . . no, a ghost, with light sifting through him, stood next to this bed last night, Uncle Ty. I swear the sleeping pill hadn't had time to kick in, and I was awake. He called himself a preacher."

Silence had hung in the air, like a thick fog, and I had ransacked my mind in an attempt to figure out what to say to Hannah. *Reverend Maynard. Why'd he appear to her?* I had held eye contact with her, and my mind had raced to come up with a reasonable answer.

"Am I crazy?" Tears had run in rivulets down my niece's cheeks.

Cancer stealing her life isn't her worst nightmare.

My niece had pulled her right hand free from my sheltered hold and placed it over her mouth. Though a grown woman, her eyes, like my sister Allison's, had had an innocence about them. And through muffled sobs, she'd said, "I love Brad. But his response after I told him about the ghost caused me to withhold something from him. Yes, I'd had anxiety about the possibility of me having cancer, but the minute Dr. Hartmann told me I didn't it left. I saw my mom in that ghost's blue eyes. I know how that sounds. But I swear it's true."

I'd leaned over and embraced her. I'd wanted to tell her that I'd had a visit from the reverend and Allison, too. I had wanted to relieve her anxiety. But to anyone's ears, her story wouldn't have sounded remotely possible. So I'd played the stress card on her, backed up Brad's notion, and I'd hated myself for doing it.

Alex had entered with a cup of coffee, and my conversation with Hannah had halted. "The others are still in the cafeteria. Everything okay?"

"Yeah, Honey. But I've worn Hannah out with all my talking."

Alex had smiled. "Better let her rest, then, Ty."

"Yeah, I'll be right out." My wife had turned and left Hannah's hospital room.

"Uncle Ty, do you believe what I told you?"

I have to lie, I'd told myself. But awareness of the wrong deed had shamed me. "I believe you think you saw a ghost. But you imagined it. I think that pill caused you to hallucinate."

"Just Brad and you know," she'd said.

And Drew. But I won't tell her.

"Brad said I shouldn't tell the doctor."

I had acknowledged a reality. Dr. Hartmann, a man of science, had dealt with facts. *My niece can't end up in a psych ward*, had flashed through my mind. "I agree with Brad. Don't mention anything about a ghost."

She'd nodded in agreement. "Thanks, Uncle Ty. I love you."

I'd left her room. A chant had reverberated in my head, *I have to protect her. I have to.* But the real reason I had lied thumped me at my core. I should have acknowledged the truth, should have admitted I've had a visit from Reverend Maynard, too.

I'm a lousy uncle.

Chapter 6 - The Chapel
Monday Morning, May 29

Alex and I had called our grandkids in New York. Since Marcus and Mindy, Robert and Lizzie's twins, hadn't quite turned five, they hadn't gotten upset about the canceled Memorial Day barbeque Grandpa T had customarily made. But their brother, Tyler, eight, and Andrea and Tom's kids, Sarah and Sam, nine and ten, had sounded disappointed. In particular, they hadn't wanted to miss our traditional Grandpa T verses the grandkids water balloon fight. Angela, pregnant and not in the best of moods, hadn't thought she and Andrew would have made it to the barbeque, anyway.

We'd walked past the inpatient waiting area, and Drew and Jenny had waved.

Hannah hadn't spoken when we'd gone in to say hi, but her fragile smile and the whites of her eyes, laced with a red web, had affirmed that she'd experienced a rough night. I'd kissed her forehead, and Alex had hugged her.

Brad had stood next to her bed. "Thanks for coming, but she isn't in a cordial mood. She had a rough night. She refused the sleeping pill last night. Can't blame her. I wouldn't have taken it, either, not after what it did to her the night before. But she couldn't sleep. Past midnight, I hit the call button and asked the nurse to give her a different pill, one not as potent. But the nurse said she needed Dr. Hartmann's authorization. Hannah insisted that the nurse shouldn't call his exchange. But when he comes by today, I'll ask him to prescribe one that isn't as strong."

Except for Brad, I and the rest of my Missouri family had settled in the waiting room. My niece's testimony about a preacher standing next to her bed had swept away my rationale that a dream had conjured up my spirit visitors. *But how can I tell my niece about my encounter and not break her heart?* I'd reasoned. Reverend Maynard had spoken to me, too. And though Hannah had seen her mother in the reverend's eyes, my niece hadn't mentioned speaking to her mother. And I had.

Hannah had needed rescuing from the fate of lung cancer. Entangled in the throes of her certain death, it had occurred to me that I hadn't followed the reverend's command, hadn't done what my sister's spirit expected of me. I'd decided to find the hospital's chapel and pray for my niece.

My wife had remained clueless about what had transpired the previous Saturday night, as we'd slept in my deceased sister's bed. And I had wanted to keep it that way. She'd have labeled my encounter a dream. *I need to thank God for gifting me with that visit from Allison and Reverend Maynard, too.* I'd decided to slip away, pray alone, and get back before the doctor had started his rounds.

"Honey," I'd said, "I think I'll check at the nurses' station to find out if Dr. Hartmann has started his rounds."

Alex had glanced at her wristwatch and squinted. "It's only six-fifteen, Ty. You're stressed out, and that makes you impatient."

Of course, she'd been right. But my opportunity to go to the chapel had been foiled. I'd remained seated and had picked up a magazine from the table next to the couch. I had flipped through it and placed it back on the table.

My wife had stood. "Let's take a walk."

We'd proceeded down the hall, out of our Missouri family's earshot. "You need to relax."

"Sorry, Alex. Besides worrying about Hannah, I'm worried about what's going on at our dance studio. We've left our instructors in charge. They're good at teaching, but they act immature sometimes. "Of course, this had rung true in her ears. And I had had those concerns. But my pressing motive, praying in the chapel alone, had driven me to exaggerate them. I had needed to have a heart-to-heart with God.

"Call Robert and set your mind at ease. He said he'd check on the studio. And when it comes to being conscientious, he's a chip off the old block," Alex had laughed.

"You're right, Honey. He is. But I want to run a promotional idea for the studio past him, too. And I don't like to discuss business in front of our Missouri family."

"Okay, I get that, Ty. I'm going to stay here and wait for Dr. Hartmann."

"Give me a buzz when he shows. I won't be gone long." I'd noted the time on my watch. As I'd entered the vacant chapel, anxiety about my niece's cancer had born down on me, and my thoughts had focused on her probable death. I had taken in a slow, deep breath to subdue my heightened state of emotion, and I'd detected a faint, sweet scent.

Distracted, I'd stopped, stood still, and looked around. I had expected to see bouquets of flowers distributed along the side walls, but none had been in sight. And as I'd approached the kneeling rail, the sweet scent had grown stronger, as if the chapel had contained cherry blossom trees in full bloom. With its floral perfume and walls painted sky blue, the chapel had reminded me of a spring day.

A brass cross had sat on the altar, and a large picture of Jesus shepherding His flock had hung on the wall above it. And like floating on a raft, with water lapping against it, all my tension had left.

In my state of calmness, I'd readied myself to do what the spirits of Reverend Maynard and my sister, Allison, had expected of me. I had lowered myself to the kneeling rail. And in my attempt to emphasize humbleness, I'd bowed my head, closed my eyes. But unable to get started, I hadn't formed a sentence, hadn't squeezed out one word. Common sense had shouted: Cancer can't be prayed away. The calmness I'd gained a moment ago had vanished. The skeptic had risen up in me and had rocked my faith. Allison's scolding had returned to me. Defeated, I'd pushed up from the kneeling rail, and my underarms had leaked sweat onto my shirt from my anxiety. Ready to succumb to failure, I'd heard, "Ask with your heart." I'd turned and looked behind me. I had expected to see a priest or the spirit of Reverend Maynard, though the regal tone hadn't matched his voice. With no clue about the communication's origin, I'd turned to face the altar again. The shape of the brass cross had morphed. Before me glowed a sphere, and it had emitted a deep, red radiance, the color of blood.

"I am the Almighty, creator of heaven and earth. You need not move your lips to speak to me. I know your thoughts. Ask and I will answer," a voice emanated from the morphing brass.

The steeled words, though commanding to my ears, had chimed of kindness in my heart. They had reinforced that He could do anything. I'd lowered myself to the rail, bowed my head, and said a simple, silent prayer: *God, please save my niece, Hannah. Amen.* And as my inner voice had released those words, the brass cross had returned to its former state. I had experienced a gift. God had graced me with a miracle.

I'd exited the chapel and given Robert a call to ease my guilty conscience about lying to Alex. His phone had gone to voicemail. *He's in class.* I had left a brief explanation about my promotional idea and asked how lessons at the studio had gone.

I had looked at my watch. *Better get back. I want to hear what Dr. Hartmann has to say.*

Alex, seated on the couch in the waiting room, had had a questioning look on her face. "Everything okay at the studio?"

Exhilaration had coursed through me, but how could I have disclosed what had happened in the chapel? Instead, I'd lied to my wife. "Yeah. You were right. Robert checked on our dance instructors. Everything's fine. And he liked my idea to promote The Silver Slipper."

Chapter 7 - The Redhead
Tuesday, May 30

I had wished I'd had a good cup of coffee. *This ink black vending machine stuff has my scalp tingling.* Drew and Jenny hadn't eaten breakfast, and they'd gone to the cafeteria to get a sandwich for an early lunch. It had occurred to me that a decent cup of coffee and at least a piece of pie accompanying it might have afforded me a better distraction from my numb backside. *I should have asked them to bring something back for Alex and me.*

The prospect that Dr. Hartmann might not show that morning, like the coffee, had grown stronger, more bitter, with each passing moment. But I'd kept my frozen rear planted for fear I would miss Hannah's doctor.

Brad hadn't left his wife's side. "Stretch your legs," I'd told him. "We'll sit with her."

"I could use a cigarette," he'd said.

We'd sat side by side next to Hannah's bed. Alex had opened her book, and I had looked at text messages on my phone. Our niece's eyelids had fluttered, and a twitch had set in her right hand. *Is she dreaming?*

Mere minutes had passed, and Brad had returned to his wife's room. He had reeked of cigarette smoke, and his swollen eyelids and gloomy face had painted a picture of hopelessness. He'd twirled his wedding band around and around his finger, as he'd done before. "Thank-you. I appreciate the break."

"You weren't gone long," Alex had said.

"Well, I don't want to miss Hannah's doctor."

Poor guy's a wreck. Alex and I had gone back to the waiting room and sat on the couch.

Like candle wax melting sluggishly away, the afternoon had slipped away from us, yet Dr. Hartmann hadn't made his rounds.

Alex had fidgeted through her purse, pulled out a bottle of Tylenol, and downed two tablets with a swig of cold coffee. Then, she'd taken out her cell phone.

"Hi Angela. How's your day going?" With the phone pressed to her ear, I had watched my wife's face transform. Her eyebrows had arched, and her forehead had wrinkled. Her eyes had scrunched into slits, and her pursed lips had formed dimples at the corners of her mouth. "Tell that old battle-axe you can't stay late. She needs to ease up. Guess The Redhead's never been pregnant." A flush had invaded my wife's cheeks and given her light complexion a fiery glow. She'd flung her left hand out in anger, like she'd swatted a pesky fly. "But . . . I'm your mother; you need your rest. Okay, I'll let you go. Yes, I'll tell him. Love you, too."

"What's up," I'd asked.

"Angela's boss is nitpicking about a fabric print she's created. I think she's afraid our daughter's a better designer than she is," Alex had said.

"Honey, Mrs. Schrader's the owner of Schrader Graphic Designs. She doesn't have to compete with an employee."

Like my wife hadn't heard me, she'd continued voicing her opinion, and her volume had gotten louder. "Seven months pregnant. And The Redhead's working her tail off. I should give that woman a piece of my mind." Alex's eyes had zeroed in on mine, and she'd released a loud exhale. "By the way, Angela sends her love."

I had had what I'd call an inward laugh. Wow. Imagine what might happen if The Redhead and my dark-haired beauty, with her father's temper, had a face-to-face.

Frustrated with the ill treatment of one of our daughters, Alex had decided she'd better check on Andrea.

"No answer, Ty."

"Leave a message. She's busy with that case. She'll get back to you."

Alex had nodded. "She always does."

Chapter 8 - Dr. Hartmann
Afternoon

Brad had come out to the waiting room, and he'd told us the nurse had started an IV. But other than that, we hadn't yielded any more enlightenment. My rump had progressed from prickly needle sticks to total numbness by afternoon. *In my lifetime I haven't sat this long*, had traipsed through my mind. And besides that, the vending machine junk food, four Twix and three Snicker bars, merged with too many cups of coffee had had my nerves vibrating. I had gotten up from the couch, in the waiting area, and walked up and down the hallway, until feeling had returned to my backside.

At 12:50 p.m., Dr. Hartmann's muscular frame had breezed past us in the waiting room. I'd tapped Drew's shoulder. He'd flinched and startled Jenny, seated next to him, and she'd dropped her crossword puzzle. The surgeon had entered Hannah's room, and we'd all followed him in. He had acknowledged us with a nod. "Looks like the whole family is present," he'd said, but his voice hadn't possessed any expression, and his face had looked like a blank sheet of paper. He'd made eye contact with Hannah. "I have your lab report. As you know, the CT scan of your chest showed an abscess inside your left lung. My concern was that the abscess could mean underlying endobronchial cancer."

My chest had tightened waiting for him to drop the big C word, my niece's new reality. Allison's spirit told me her daughter had cancer. But . . . I did what Reverend Maynard told me to do. I prayed.

Dr. Hartmann had smiled. "But I'm happy to tell you the report indicates there's no cancer. The culture of the abscess showed the presence of streptococcal infection."

"Strep throat?" Hannah had said.

The tension in my body had released. But important questions had registered. *How'd it get in her left lung? And how long till she's rid of it? I hope Brad asks.*

"You inhaled the streptococci bacteria into your lungs, and that caused the abscess. I'm going to give you an antibiotic through an IV. You didn't complain about a sore throat, Hannah. And that stumped me," Dr. Hartmann had said.

"Well . . . I didn't think I had a sore throat, but I've felt tired."

The doctor had shaken his head as if puzzled, then he'd pulled up Hannah's chart on the computer mounted on the wall. His eyes had followed the notes entered by the nurses. "Your temperature has run at ninety-nine degrees, but that's normal for some people. I'll be right back," the doctor had said. He'd returned with a nurse.

"I need to take your temperature," the nurse had said, and placed the thermometer on my niece's forehead. "Ninety-nine point nine, Dr. Hartmann."

"Get Hannah some ibuprofen, adjust the bed for postural drainage, and set up an IV for Cefpirome."

The nurse had adjusted my niece's bed and then hurried out of Hannah's room.

"I'm sorry I didn't get to tell you the good news about your report sooner," Dr. Hartmann had said. "Cancer is a frightening word. I started my rounds this morning, and two emergency surgeries came in, one after the other." As if he'd straightened his hair, he had run his hand along the side of his bald head. "The antibiotic in your IV line needs to stay in for two days. If there's no fever Thursday, I'll discharge you and write you a script for an oral antibiotic. Finish all of it. How's that sound?"

Like rays of sunshine had permeated a gloomy cloud, Hannah's face had brightened, and the corners of her lips had turned up and formed a smile. "Great! My little Rachel misses me."

"I want to see you in my office two weeks from Thursday. Any questions?"

Tears of joy had trickled down Hannah's cheeks. "No. And thank-you, Dr. Hartmann."

In the quiet of my thoughts, I'd said, *My niece's cancer no longer exists. Thank-you God.* But I'd understood the reality. If Allison hadn't told me to pray for Hannah, malignant cells could have stolen her life, like a thief.

I had visualized the family pictures that hung on the wall in our home office. *The omens warned me. But is Hannah's picture on it? Pretend I'm sitting at my desk. Concentrate. Start in the center. Our wedding picture. Okay. Work my way out. Anniversary photos of our parents. Second circle. Robert and*

Lizzie, with Tyler, Marcus, and Mindy. Third. Andrea and Tom, with Sarah and Sam. And this circle continues with pictures of Angela and Andrew. Fill in the perimeter, I'd prodded my memory. My mind's eye had produced a small photo. *Allison, Drew, and yes, their daughter, Hannah, much younger.* A wave of sadness had washed over me, and I'd closed my eyes. *Allison, they did a great job raising her. Jenny's a good woman, and she loves them both. Your family's in good hands.*

I'd breathed a sigh of relief. *The omen's predictions are satisfied.* But in the next second, a whisper inside my head had said, *No. Not yet.*

Chapter 9 - Andrea's Case
Evening

At 6:15, past Dad's supper time, he had barreled down the highway, ridding the dividing line. My right foot had borne down on the backseat floor for the brake pedal. *Why didn't I suggest getting dinner in the hospital's cafeteria? Or at least offer to drive? No, that would've insulted him.*

Alex's cell phone had rung.

"It's Andrea," my wife had mouthed to me. "Hi Sweetheart." After a pause, she'd said, "That's okay. I knew you'd get back to me."

As a prosecutor for the District Attorney's Vehicular Crimes Unit, our daughter had provided legal assistance to help NYPD case detectives prosecute drunk, drugged, and reckless drivers.

"Put her on speakerphone," I'd mouthed.

"How's the case going?" Alex had asked.

"Okay. And that's all I'll say about it, Mom." A gusty huff had come through the phone. "I'm not allowed to divulge evidence!"

Dad had turned his neck, and his frown had said clear as words what he'd thought about Andrea's answer to her mother.

"I understand," Alex had said. "There's a code of ethics you're sworn to abide by. And I respect that. I didn't mean to upset you. But I'm worried about you."

I'd taken Alex's phone from her. "Andrea, you're allowing this case to get to you. Hand it off to another lawyer. You've helped the other lawyers out, before."

"Dad, I stood next to Detective Barrows and witnessed the police taking pictures of the bicyclist's dead body. I saw and heard other things I can't tell you about. But I'll tell you this, the man had a family. And I'm going to do my best to give them the only closure I can offer them, a court judgement of Vehicular Manslaughter. And that's still a rotten deal for his wife and kids."

"Read your newspaper. You'll get an account of what happened, what caused the collision," Andrea had said. "But whether or not it's true . . . well, we'll have to wait and see."

Chapter 10 - Greenstone Church
Later in the Evening

Dad had trimmed ten minutes off of our ride from Barnes-Jewish Hospital to Greenstone. At 7:05 p.m., we'd parked on my folks' sparsely graveled driveway.

We'd finished supper, scrambled eggs and ham, then sat in the living room. Mom, talkative as usual, had dominated the conversation. Dad had put in his two cents, and Alex had talked about our grandchildren in New York. I'd pretended to listen. But like dissipating fog, their conversation had faded, and the event of the previous night had stolen my attention. *Will Reverend Maynard's and Allison's spirits return? Wish I had apologized. Asked for her forgiveness.*

I'd thought the night air and exercise might help lighten my mood. I had stood. "I'm going for a walk."

"I'll go with you," Alex had said. "Too much sitting at the hospital."

"Great," I'd said and tried to sound enthusiastic. Dusk had set in. "I'll get a flashlight. Still in the kitchen drawer, next to the stove, Mom?"

"Yes," she'd smiled.

This was one of those times I'd wanted to mull things over by myself. I'd had a specific destination in mind, but no understanding of why the old wooden church, where Reverend Maynard had preached, beckoned me. *Didn't attend much as a kid. Alex and I attended once. And that was with my folks.*

"Where are we going?" Alex had said.

"Nowhere in particular." *Wish she had stayed with my parents.*

The right side of my face had served as Alex's focal point, and I hadn't made eye contact with her. I had supposed what she would have said if I'd told her my destination. And I hadn't had an answer.

She'd stopped walking. "Hannah doesn't have cancer, and we're going home Thursday. But I can tell you're uptight. Why?"

"I don't know. Sorry, Alex."

"You need time alone, to unwind. I'm tired, anyway. I'll go back and read."

I had turned on the flashlight and handed it to her. "Thanks for understanding, Honey."

"She'd kissed me. "Sure. Love you."

By my estimate, we had walked three-quarters of a mile on the gravel road, and it was a straight shot back to my parents' house. I would never have let Alex walk one block at night alone in New York for fear she'd get robbed or abducted. But in Greenstone, a person could have taken a walk at midnight. I'd turned and watched the curvature of light as her hand swung like a pendulum, to and fro.

A rush of anticipation had hit me, like when I'd gotten antsy to open Christmas presents as a kid and discover what treasures I'd received. My swift steps had transformed to a jog. My shoes had struck the jagged gravel with force and jabbed pain into the soles of my feet. I'd finished the last quarter of a mile in no time, but an awareness had dampened my eagerness. *It's a weekday. And it's nighttime. But folks in Greenstone don't lock their doors. Maybe it's open.*

All four wooden steps had flexed from my weight. A bulb above the two doors had emitted a faint, yellow light. I'd braced my hands against the frame of one of the narrow windows and tried to look inside. But the sliver of moon and the yellow bulb hadn't cast enough light to make out the interior.

My attention had returned to the church's double door entrance. I'd taken hold of the tarnished doorknob on the right, turned it, and pushed in on the door with my left. Locked.

My mission aborted, I'd turned to leave. *Why'd I decide to come here in the first place?* That's when a voice inside my head had whispered, *Try the left door; it's open.* Drained from worry and a long day at the hospital, I had needed to vent my frustration. For the heck of it, I'd leaned into the door, turned the knob, and pushed with all the force I had. And it had opened. I had stepped inside, and the door closed behind me.

It's pitch-black. Should have brought my phone. How will I find the light switch? No, I had remembered. *Pull chains. Along the side walls.* With my right arm outstretched and my hand as a feeler, I'd shuffled along, and my shoes caught on the coarse wooden planks. I'd stopped, stood still, and reconsidered. *Maybe I should come back in the morning.*

One of the planks had creaked and broken the silence. "Who's here?" No one had answered. My heart had pounded, and beads of sweat formed above my upper lip. I'd stood still with clenched fists and listened. *A robber? Nah. The few times I'd attended, I didn't see anything valuable. That's old wood groaning.*

With the wall as my roadmap, I had moved on, until my hand hit a pull chain. I'd put it into motion. My hungry hands had chased it and grabbed at air until I caught it. I'd pulled down on the chain, and the yellow glow provided me enough light to find four more.

An aisle had separated two sets of wooden pews. I'd chosen the set closer to the lights and sat in the second pew. The plain pulpit, with a coarse, wooden cross on the front, had sparked my memory. And in my mind's eye I had visualized the rawboned Reverend Maynard preaching his sermon, years before. I had remembered how his words in a nutshell had painted the broken relationship between me and my dad. And in the next moment, the best of that memory had come back to me, the warmth of my dad's embrace, the cleansing that had wiped away the rift between us. *All that bitterness because I chose dancing instead of mining. But what about Allison? How can I wipe that slate clean?*

My sister had appeared, sitting next to me in the pew, as if my thoughts had beckoned her. She'd smiled. "Thank-you for praying, Bird." Like Reverend Maynard, her eyes had served as the medium for speech. "Shed your guilt. I wouldn't have gone with you if you had asked. I belonged in Greenstone. You didn't. I'm glad you pursued your career in New York." A light touch, as though her fingers had brushed across my cheek, had brought tears to my eyes, and she'd vanished. *No! Don't go,* the words had screamed inside my head. *There are things I need to say.* And a question had jabbed at my heart. *What if I don't see her again?*

Chapter 11 - Ty Meets P.J.
Wednesday Morning, May 31

Mom, Dad, Alex, and I had arrived at the hospital around 9:30. Brad had joined us in the waiting room. "The nurse is hooking up another bag of that antibiotic for the strep infection. She has to get Hannah's vitals, too. Then you can go in. But the nurse said one person at a time."

"So glad things turned out the way they did," I'd said. "Mom and Dad, Alex, you guys each take a turn visiting with Hannah, and I'll go in last. I'd better call the airport and book a flight." *Sure hope I get one for tomorrow.* I had pulled out my phone and dialed as I'd walked down the hall.

Like someone had nudged me toward the elevator, I'd pressed the button and entered. And as if someone had directed my hand, I'd pushed the button for the Main Floor. When the door opened, I'd understood where I had to go, but not why.

I'd stood at the doorway and looked inside. Not empty this time. *I'll sit in the pew closest to the door.* A man with thick auburn hair two rows in front of me had his head bowed. His shoulders had risen and fallen. His head had shaken in short rapid movements. *He's bawling.* I'd gotten up to leave, and my size twelve shoe struck the leg of the pew and cut through the silence. The man had turned around and looked at me. His face, a blotchy red mess, had confirmed my one assumption, but his thick auburn hair had deceived me. *Poor guy needs privacy.* I'd proceeded to leave.

"Wait," the man had said, "don't go, please."

I'd taken in his eyelids, drooped in crinkled folds, and the puffy sacks beneath his eyes, certain death of a loved one had caused his pathetic appearance. And with those deep parentheses running from the bottom of his nose to the corners of his mouth, he'd looked like one sad, old man. His misery had reached out to me, but with no clue what to say, I had hesitated. And in that uncomfortable silence, the man had used his hand to wipe at his eyes. "Do you need help, Sir?" I'd asked and proceeded to the pew where he'd sat.

He'd stood, faced me. "It's my wife. She's in the ICU. The doctor said she's not going to . . . make it. Today, maybe tomorrow. That's all she has left. Your wife in here, too?"

"No, my niece."

"Sorry to hear that."

"Well, we got good news. She gets to go home tomorrow." *He's past eighty*. My eyes had taken in the gold band on his left hand. Chills had spread through my body at the thought of living without Alex.

The elderly man had attempted to smile. "That's wonderful."

"Is there someone I can call to be with you?"

"No, we don't have children, and her sister, her only sibling, died from leukemia, too. Three years ago."

"Friends?"

"Helen's lady friends are in assisted living. My buddy died two years ago. It's just me and her. There's nobody else. Would you mind praying with me?"

His request had taken me by surprise. But as I had tried to grasp what a mess I'd be if Alex was in his wife's predicament, I had understood with my heart. *Helen's his whole life.*

"Please?"

"Well," I'd hesitated, "okay."

We'd made our way to the kneeling rail. I had lowered myself, but the elderly man had paused. He'd looked up at the picture of Jesus shepherding his sheep, then he'd knelt, too. I had bowed my head, closed my eyes, and waited, then waited some more. And when I'd opened my eyes, the man had been looking back at me. "Well, I'm ready if you are. Go ahead," I'd said. "Haven't done it for a long time. My folks took me to church as a kid, and I believe, but I thought maybe you had more practice praying. My Helen doesn't believe in God, and I'm worried about her soul. Maybe you're better connected with Him."

Poor old guy. His wife's on her deathbed, and he thinks I can help get her into heaven?' By the way, I'm Ty. What's your name?"

"P.J.," he'd said and stuck out his hand. His cold fingers, knotty as the trunk of an old oak tree, had surprised me with a strong grip.

"Okay, P.J. I'll give it a shot, but I'm no expert."

We had bowed our heads. "God, Helen's doctor told P. J. she's going to pass soon. But you're the one in charge of life and death.

Someone told me that if we ask You for help, You always give an answer. We're asking You to heal Helen. But if she isn't meant to get well, please help her find faith, somehow let her know You. P. J. wants to see her again in heaven. In Jesus name we pray. Amen."

He'd pushed himself up from the kneeling rail. "Thank-you, Ty. God bless you."

"I'm not family, but maybe I could sneak in the ICU and check on you and Helen. What's your last name?"

"Monroe. And I'd sure appreciate that."

I'd watched P.J. exit the chapel. His aged body had swayed from side to side, and he'd moved at a slow gait.

I had walked toward the exit, but I'd stopped at the doorway. I'd looked back at the picture above the altar, and my phone had vibrated. I'd taken it out of my pocket and turned up the volume. "Hi, Honey. What's up?"

"We've all visited with Hannah. She'd like to speak with you."

"I'm on my way."

My niece had smiled when I'd entered her room. "Hi." I'd said. "You're looking perky today."

"After Dr. Hartmann told me I don't have cancer . . . it felt like someone had lifted a heavy weight off of me."

"I understand. And I'm so happy for you."

"But Uncle Ty," she'd spoken in a whisper, "that old man with the white goatee, the ghost I told you about, he let me have a glimpse of my deceased mother. I didn't hallucinate. And I didn't dream it, either." Her eyes had remained locked on mine.

Lie to her again, or tell her the truth? How can I tell her I spoke with Allison? She didn't. It would break her heart. "As I said before, I agree with Brad. That pill conjured up a hallucination. And if I were you, I wouldn't bring up this ghost business again with Brad or the rest of the family. You want to go home tomorrow, don't you?"

Hannah had managed a defeated nod of compliance. And my dishonesty had attacked my conscience. *What if the Reverend or Allison visits her, again? She'll for sure think she's crazy. I'm a heel.*

Chapter 12 - Home
Thursday Morning, June 1

Our cab driver had dropped us off at home, and he'd waited with the meter running. Antsy to check on our studio, we'd hauled our luggage inside and grabbed a cup of coffee to revitalize us from our early flight.

Alex and I had entered The Silver Slipper, and one of my all-time favorite songs had been playing. I'd looked at my watch. *Intermediate swing is in session.*

My wife had gone into the office. Drawn to the music, I'd peeked through the glass window in Ballroom One. Our full-time dance instructors, Ethan and Olivia, had been demonstrating the kick-ball-change, a syncopated move requiring two weight changes in three beats.

Ethan had stopped the DVD player. "Now, watch and listen while Olivia and I break the dance step down. We start in open position, facing each other, like so. I'll start with my left foot. Olivia will start with her right. On count one, the man kicks from the knee with his left foot, pointing his toe out in front of him, so it clears the floor. On count two, he places the ball of his left foot back in contact with the floor, like he's tapping it. Count three, he steps in place with the right foot. And on count four, he puts his weight back on his left. Now, the man can lead another kick-ball-change or move onto a different step."

Ethan had waved at me and Alex, then he'd turned to Olivia. "Go through the steps with the ladies. Then have the couples practice the kick-ball-change as you call out the man's steps. I'll be right back."

"Hey, good to see you, Ty. Everything okay with your niece?"

"Yeah. She's doing great. Going home today. Thanks for asking. How's your day going?"

"For the most part, fine."

"But you've run into a problem?"

"Yeah. The old guy in Basic Swing, the one with the big belly. He got on his partner's nerves. Occupied with helping another couple, I didn't see what he did. But I sure heard his partner scream, 'Stop it!' And she ran out of the ballroom."

Henry. "Thanks for telling me. I know who you mean. I'll speak with him."

A mellow tune we'd used for teaching beginner's waltz had sifted through the wall separating the two ballrooms. "Guess I'll drop in and say hi to Nick and Kayla."

Ethan had arched his eyebrows and alerted me of my slip-up. "Ty, they had classes at the university. They couldn't help today."

"Yeah, that's right. Got my days mixed-up." *My niece's health. Her visits with the Reverend and my sister's spirits. I need to catch up on my sleep.*

"It was good that Robert took a few personal days to help out," Ethan had said. "He's teaching the class. Alex didn't come with you?"

"She's in the office. Thanks for taking care of the studio."

"You're welcome."

I'd headed to Ballroom Two.

"One-two-three, one-two-three," Robert had counted out the beat for the basic waltz step.

He'd paused. "Hi, Dad. Hey, I called Brad earlier, and he put Hannah on the phone. She sounded good. Glad things turned out the way they did."

"Yeah, we all are." I'd embraced Robert. "You shouldn't have used your personnel days."

"After all you guys did for me? I'll never forget those afternoons I spent with you and Mom at The Silver Slipper. I couldn't wait for kindergarten to end. My afternoons at the studio planted the seed for my profession. I love this place. I'll help you anyway I can. Don't ever hesitate to ask, okay?"

"Okay. Thanks, Son."

Alex had entered holding a paper bag. "Hi, Robert. What are you doing here?"

"Used a few of my personal days. And I thoroughly enjoyed teaching at my former stomping ground. Whatcha got there, Mom?"

"Bills and vendors' catalogues. I need to order different dance shoes for our boutique. Our students must not like the styles we carry."

That's not the problem, popped into my head. *Enrollment's down. Most of our older, long-standing students stayed, but the younger ones have gone to the newer studios.*

"Can you get the order done while I talk to Robert? I want to discuss my promotional idea for the studio."

Our son's eyes had lit up with interest.

"Ty, I tagged along to listen to our messages and go through the mail. I have laundry to do. Discuss your idea. I'll catch the next train home."

I don't want her riding alone. "On second thought, I'll go with you. I'm worn out." *True, at least.*

Robert had smiled. "Dad, we could meet at the studio Saturday morning. Around ten? I'm free. How about you?"

"Sounds great."

Chapter 13 - Henry
Friday, June 2

Alex and I had been teaching beginner's East Coast Swing, the style of dance I'd learned as a teenager in Greenstone. It had influenced me to choose dancing as my career. Unfortunately, Henry had shown up. *He has his nerve*, had coursed through my mind and heated my face.

The goal Alex and I had set for the day's lesson was to introduce a new move, the Hully Gully. We had wanted to build onto a sequence we'd taught in the previous lesson. But first, as usual, we'd had the ladies and men partner up for a review. Henry had grabbed Marie, a looker in her thirties, with long, dark hair. The woman Ethan had said left class crying. *How could Henry think she wanted to dance with him again? Why would any of the women want to?*

I had positioned Alex and me with an unobstructed view of Henry.

"Due to mine and Alex's absence this week, I want to review the closed dance position and the basic six-count step taught by the two Adelphi students who filled in for us. Watch my wife and I demonstrate them first." I had faced Alex, placed my right hand on the left side of her waist, and I'd taken hold of her right hand with my left. "Ladies, like Alex has shown, her left-hand rests on my right shoulder."

I had checked their holds. "Good. We'll do a walk-through review of the basic step. Men, start with your left foot, ladies with your right. I'll count out the beats, one and two, three and four, and the rock step."

Most of the students had done well. Henry hadn't led Marie well. *He's too clumsy to dance. I wish he'd drop out.*

"Good," I'd said. *Except for Henry.* "Let's move on to a Sweetheart Wrap." I'd taken Alex in hold again. "The man lifts his left hand while holding his lady's right, and he turns her around in front of him to his right side for an outside turn. The man does counts one and two in place, like so, and raises his left hand over his lady's head, leading her on counts three and four into his right arm with an inside, half-counterclockwise turn. She now is in a Sweetheart Wrap. Gentlemen, you should be looking at the back of your lady's head. Hold her in this wrap. Alex and I are going to teach you an additional move called the hully gully. Men–"

That's when I'd heard, "Henry, stop it!"

My line of sight had shot toward Marie. I'd taken in her tearful eyes and the panic displayed on her face. *He's pulled her back too far, and her rear end is against his fly.* "Henry, release her!"

Marie had turned, slapped his face, and had run out of the ballroom. Alex had gone after her.

Henry's vulgar lack of respect had struck a nerve. Anger had heated my face and snaked down my neck. And I had approached him and stood a hairsbreadth from his face. "I've confronted you before about your shenanigans, and the instructor who handled this class in my absence reported your inappropriateness, too."

"That young punk doesn't have any patience with the elderly, either."

"Get out and *don't* show your face here again." He'd stood his ground with a smirk of superiority on his face. The bulbous sacks beneath his eyes had pulsated, and his protruded belly had jiggled, as if in sync with his raucous laughter. I had looked down on his squatty body. "Get out, or I'm calling the police!"

His face had turned cherry red. He'd taken a clumsy step backward, spread his feet apart, into what had looked like a boxer's stance, and his big gut had hung in rounded lumps, like a sagging sack of potatoes. He'd narrowed his eyes, pursed his lips.

Alex had returned and put her hand on my arm, as if she'd thought I might take him up on his challenge. "Well, Henry," she'd said, "Marie left and isn't coming back. You should be ashamed. It's no wonder none of the ladies want to dance with you."

Henry's line of sight had dropped to his shoes. "Old people get mixed up when you give them too many directions. Do this, do that. On and on it goes. It's too much to remember." His labored breathing had shaken his big belly.

Sly old fox thinks I believe that. "You're a bad actor, Henry."

Alex had smiled at the old guy, but not the way she'd smiled at me through the years. "You'll act like a gentleman and follow directions from now on or Ty and I will refuse to give you lessons."

No, Alex. Don't let him stay.

"Another one that's full of herself." Henry's eyes had turned glassy. He'd picked up his street shoes and headed toward the door. But before he'd exited the ballroom, he'd turned back and shouted, "From now on you both address me as Doctor Walsh."

I had turned to Alex. "He'd better not show his face here, again. Doctor? Of what?"

Chapter 14 - Ty's Vision
Saturday Morning, June 3

Alex had stayed home to get the cleaning and laundry done. I'd worked in the office to catch up on paperwork before Robert arrived.

Can't wait to tell him about my idea to promote the dance studio. But in the next second, a dark cloud had burst through my sunshine. Reality had hit, and negative thoughts washed away my excitement. *Neither of our ballrooms is a good venue. Lighting's bad. Poor acoustics. And what about seating? Tacky folding chairs? Costumes and makeup? Who's doing that? Robert will put his heart into this.* And like those considerations had opened the door to what I'd deemed a disaster, I had come to a decision. *I don't want to waste his time. My son's a professional. I'm not ruining his reputation with an amateur production.*

Our son had arrived with a big smile on his face. "Hi, Dad. Can't wait to hear about your idea."

"After thinking about it, I've decided not to have the promotional performance."

"Why? I've been salivating trying to guess what you have up your sleeve. Run it past me anyway."

My instinct to tell him the truth had gotten swallowed up by my ego. *It won't hurt to get his opinion.* "Honest feedback?"

"You know I don't sugarcoat my opinions when it comes to dance."

That's true. "Well, I ran across a book your mom and I bought last year at the Botanic Cherry Blossom Festival. And I remembered the Japanese belief that the blossoms go through a cycle of life, death, and renewal, like humans. I want to humanize the Japanese cherry blossoms. Get the audience connected emotionally. Get them to experience the blossoms' story as a mirror of their own destiny. And I'd thought, here's a story dance movements can tell."

The look on Robert's face had spoken to me before he'd responded. "I like it, Dad! And what about the setting?"

"An elderly Japanese grandmother in a park, telling her young grandson a story about life's journey for cherry blossoms. But in reality, her goal is to teach him about the frailty and mortality of human life."

My son's eyes had lit up, and he'd smiled. "Contemporary dance and ballet?"

"That's what's I thought, too, Robert."

"Wow, love it! An emotional story the audience connects with. We'll bring them to their feet teary-eyed, thundering with applause, latching onto a loved one. How could you have doubted the merits of something like this? I'm all in." My son had embraced me. "We'll call the performance, *Dance of Cherry Blossoms*. And Dad, I have a friend who can build the framework for a tree, with footholds strong enough to hold dancers."

"I like your ideas," I had said. But my previous concerns I'd had before intruded on this happy moment. "But The Silver Slipper isn't a suitable venue."

"You're right. This gem deserves a stage, professional lighting, good acoustics, and a quality sound system," Robert had said.

"I agree. That's why I've decided not to go forward with it."

"Dad, I'm part of the dance faculty at Adelphi University of Performing Arts. Our campus on Long Island has a great dance theatre. You and Mom recruit the five best students enrolled in your contemporary or ballet classes. If they're in both, that's better. I'll handpick students from my classes, too. That way I can slant the performance as publicity for the university and avoid the rental fee."

With Robert in the performance, we'll wow the audience, had surged through my mind. *And him on stage with Alex and me will rank as one of the best moments of my life. I don't need to tell him enrollment has dropped. He filled-in while Alex and I went to Greenstone. He's aware.*

"I won't mention Adelphi as a possible venue to your mother. If you're given a green light, you tell her."

"I'll make it happen, Dad, and practices must start right away. A lot of events get booked in the PAC theatre when the fall session starts. We need to move on this. Otherwise, open dates are limited. Can you and Mom have your dancers chosen by Wednesday?"

"Yes. I have ones in mind. We have talented students in our Contemporary and Ballet classes." *I hope they remain our students.*

"Good. Will you and Mom put together the screening movements?"

"Of course."

"Practices Monday through Thursday nights, 5:30 to 7:30? Saturdays 9:00 till noon?"

"Sounds good."

"Great. I'll check with my colleague, Brandon Lutz, and try to get him on board as production manager. He'll get students majoring in design and technology to handle the costumes, lighting, sound system, and video projection. And he's a great guy to work with."

"Okay. Thanks, Son." My conscience had clobbered me a second time. *He'll spend hours recruiting and organizing. He has work of his own and a family. It isn't right to add more to his plate.*

"By the way, I won't dance in the performance."

"What? Why? You're a better dancer than me or your mother."

"No. I'm not. And the goal of this performance, promoting The Silver Slipper, must showcase Alexandra and Ty Partridge.

"I'll take care of the publicity, Dad. My students will post flyers at Adelphi University and at any local businesses that will allow us to. I'll check on posting a notice on www.LongIsland.com Weekly Newsletter. And I'll get a local newspaper reporter to attend *Dance of Cherry Blossoms*. Allow me to handle the programs, too. Besides the regular information about the dancers and stages of life they represent, I'll write a bio about you and Mom. How you're owners of The Silver Slipper, how you each have more than thirty-three years of dancing experience. Okay?"

"Sounds great! But that's a lot of work."

"No. It isn't. The Silver Slipper is where you and Mom taught me to dance. Robert had taken a deep breath. "I have the perfect woman in mind for the storyteller, too. She's an instructor in the dance department, also. And Tyler would jump at the chance to join you and Mom on stage. He could play the grandson. Sound good?"

"Sounds great! But Robert, I want you in the performance. I haven't been honest. Stressed what's at stake. Our enrollment has taken a dive the last three sessions. I've had to get into our savings to pay the bills."

"Is Mom aware?"

"Of fewer students, yes. But I've downplayed it as a temporary slump. I told her we'll pull out of it. But I don't think we can. A new studio opened, and their upscale facility has hurt our business."

"I'm sorry. But I'm confident about this performance. I'll promote it and do my best to draw a big crowd. Maybe it'll draw new students to your studio and bring back previous ones. I'll include registration details for lessons at The Silver Slipper in the program."

"If *Dance of Cherry Blossoms* doesn't increase enrollment, I'll tell Alex about our studio's low cash flow, Robert. But for now, let's keep this between us."

"Okay. But The Silver Slipper isn't going to close. I won't let it."

I'd smiled at my son's optimism, at his love for Alex and me, at his love for our studio. "I'll give you a copy of an outline I've put together. It tells the Japanese Cherry Blossom story."

In the quiet of my mind a prayer had formed. *God, my son's on board to help me save the studio. But to do it, we need You on board, too.*

Chapter 15 - A Look at the Dancers' Abilities
Wednesday, June 7

Classes had ended at The Silver Slipper at 5:30. I'd heard Robert in the hall telling our full-time instructors, Kayla and Nick, goodbye.

He had entered the office, smiled, and greeted Alex and me with hugs. "The chair of the dance department, Myra Randal, called me back today, and a date is set for us to meet. With Adelphi dance students in the performance and all the advertising I intend to do, we're promoting Adelphi University. I'm sure we'll get permission to use the PAC's theatre."

"I'll keep my fingers crossed, Son."

He'd handed Alex and me each a copy of the script to look over, as if we'd been given a green light already. "Mark any changes you want made. And by the way, Tyler's excited to perform on stage with you guys. And my colleague, Michaela, has committed to the storyteller/grandmother part. We'll assign the dancers their cherry blossom age category after we check their skill level. It's funny how my students keep looking younger to me," Robert had said. "Makes me feel old."

Alex had smiled. "Not near as young as a kindergartner your dad and I once had."

He had laughed, "Yeah, I was a handful, Mom."

"No. You were the best student we had."

My thoughts had pedaled backward. And my inner voice had whispered, *You loved watching our classes, loved imitating dance moves your mom and I taught. Your determination to learn surpassed that of many of our students.* "I bet Tyler's going to be a chip off the old block, Robert."

"He might. My fatherly instinct leans toward believing it's a possibility, but I've decided to not push him towards dancing as a career. He's ten and has plenty of time to decide what profession he wants. You guys gave me the opportunity to learn, but you didn't push. That's the best way, and I appreciated you for it. Thank-you. Hey, if you guys decide you want any modifications to the script, tell me as soon as possible. Okay?"

Alex had responded. "I love it as it is."

"Me too," I'd said.

"Good. Did you have a list of the contemporary and ballet moves you want used to screen the dancers tonight?"

I'd handed Robert his copy. "Yes, and they're listed next to the appropriate age category."

"You don't know how happy I am that you're in this performance," Alex had said.

"Mom. I'm not dancing."

Alex's crimson complexion had spoken louder than her verbal reply, "What?"

"This performance is about you and Dad. Promoting The Silver Slipper. My job's to oversee. Make sure things come together."

Alex hadn't said anything more, but her eyes had darted to me.

We'd heard talking in the hall. Our son had turned, motioned to two young women and a guy. "Come in. These are my three recruits, Mom and Dad. Kami," he'd pointed, "Lauren, and Matt. All three versed in contemporary and ballet."

Alex's face had returned to its normal color. "Thank-you for agreeing to perform in *Dance of Cherry Blossoms*."

"Sure," Kami had said. "We appreciate the opportunity." Matt and Lauren had nodded in agreement.

The three Adelphi students had followed us into Ballroom One. And our students from The Silver Slipper, Stephanie, Amy, Lisa, Dave, and Brian, had introduced themselves to Robert's dancers.

"Dad, please explain to the dancers what you want to communicate to the audience."

"I want us to convey the life cycle of the Japanese cherry blossom flower from its birth, or bud stage, to its death. And by humanizing the flowers, I want the audience to experience the parallel between the flowers' and humans' lives. And their eventual fates, death."

Alex, Robert, and I had demonstrated the specified modern dance and ballet movements for each stage of the cherry blossoms life: innocence of the bud, playfulness of the young, teen awareness, adult responsibility, and the ultimate destiny of the elderly, feebleness and death. The troupe had auditioned, parts had been assigned, and the dancers received their practice schedule.

After the dancers had left, Robert had taken me aside, patted me on the back. "Dad, this performance is going to bring the house down. And it'll boost enrollment at The Silver Slipper. I'm willing to bet money on it."

I had marveled at our son's enthusiasm, his confidence, but doubted it would increase enough to allow Alex and I to make a decent living.

Our son had approached Alex, who had hung back to converse with some of the girls. He'd given her a hug. "Love you, Mom. See you tomorrow night."

A deep sense of pride had overcome me, and I'd had to stifle my emotion. *Don't have much money. But God, you've blessed me with a great family.*

Chapter 16 - The Painting
Saturday, June 10

Our practice for *Dance of Cherry Blossoms* had finished at noon. "I want to do something fun today," Alex had said.

I'd rather go home and relax. Our schedule had gotten hectic due to teaching and practices for the performance at Adelphi. "I'd like to get a new painting for the living room," she'd said.

Oh, no. That could take all day. But I don't want to disappoint her. She doesn't complain about practices.

The stench of hot brake pads had filled my nose, as we'd gotten off the train. We had climbed the steps to street level at the intersection of Spring Street and Sixth Avenue in SoHo. Lower Manhattan's overcast sky, dotted with slate color clouds, had looked as if it could weep any moment, and thunder had grumbled like a constipated, old man.

For any tourist, the cast iron architecture and Belgian blocks that had paved the street would have been a treat. But I hadn't wanted to spend the rest of my day off looking for an oil painting signed by some unknown artist, unknown at least to me. And the idea of getting soaked to find this "one of a kind," as Alex had put it, had made my wife's mission more unpleasant.

I hope this doesn't take all day. Be patient. Give her time to look.

My wife had smiled, "I won't spend a lot."

I'd smiled back and hugged her. The last time we'd shopped, a pair of jeans had cost me three hundred and-twenty-five dollars.

I had swung the umbrella and picked up my pace. Alex's enthusiasm to find the perfect painting had cultivated a spring in her gait. She'd woven in and out around the crowd of weekend shoppers. And I had tried to avoid bumping into anyone. In awe of my wife's quick maneuvers, I'd looked down at her feet. *Ah, tennis shoes. No stylish, strappy sandals today.*

Several hours later, we had browsed through Sam Edelman, Alex's favorite shoe store, Chanel, her favorite perfume boutique, and numerous art galleries. And all the paintings' swirled shapes and angles had reminded me of inescapable mazes. I'd wanted to catch the subway and go home, but she hadn't finished combing southwestern Manhattan for the perfect work of art. And I hadn't wanted to leave her alone.

My wife's eyes had lit up as we'd approached a building on Broadway and Prince. The brown canopy above the entrance read: Martin Ross Gallery. "I want to go in here, Ty. I looked at this gallery's website, and they have beautiful impressionistic paintings."

"Great." *Even if it's abstract and I don't understand it, I'll pretend I do. At least we can go home.*

A white bolt of lightning had sliced through the gray streaked sky, and a loud crack of thunder, like cymbals, had struck. And I'd thought, *Bad omens.*

I had followed Alex as she'd zigzagged around people and made a beeline for the art gallery's door. A sharp pain had coursed through the side of my left foot. "That's right, cut me off," the woman had shouted. I had limped into the gallery.

The beautiful wood floor, expensive track lighting, and majestic white pillars had sent a message. *This is going to be expensive.*

"Look Ty." She'd pointed to an abstract with splatters of red, yellow, and blue displayed on an easel. "How do you like this one?"

"That's a waste of canvas."

"Shush." Then in a whisper, "Don't you see the statement?"

"No, but if you want it, buy it."

Alex 's warm brown eyes had widened, "Doesn't it stir your emotions?"

"You and dancing do that."

My wife had moved with intention, her eyes had flitted from one painting to another. Then like the sky had parted and exposed heaven, she'd stopped, and her eyes had widened in awe. "This is it!"

Good. Even if I don't like it, I'll say I do. Anything's better than the other one she likes. At first glance, I'd thought, *Okay, the artist painted a hazy, rainy day. And there's water and landscape. I can live with that.*

A man dressed in what I had judged to be an expensive suit had approached and smiled at Alex. "I'm Stephan, one of the art consultants for Martin Roland Gallery."

The way he had pronounced his name, drawn it out, as though he'd come from a royal bloodline had struck me with the certainty I'd walk out with a light wallet.

"Gorgeous, isn't it?" The consultant had said.

Alex had smiled. "Beautiful. I love impressionism art. The blurred lines remind me of our imperfect world."

"Yes," Stephan had smiled. "And this artist gives enough information to tantalize, but he leaves the viewer sorting out the painting's total meaning."

Alex had moved closer, zeroed in on the painter's scribbled signature. By the look on her face, I'd guessed she had deciphered it. "How much?"

Minutes had passed. I'd listened to the art consultant's spiel, his determination to make his commission. After he had complimented Alex's good taste, I had zoned out and backed off to let my wife dicker about the price. Like I really believed she'd get it reduced.

While I'd waited, I had examined the painting from my new vantage point. *Well, a man's sitting in a wooden rowboat. He's looking back over his shoulder toward the front of it. The cord strap of his brimmed hat and his shirttail stream toward the back of the boat. So, it's windy. The diagonal lines show heavy rain. And the man's oars can't keep the whitecaps from hurling into the boat. The blurred features of his face leave me clueless about his age. But his predicament is clear. He's trying to get to the shoreline, in the distance, to save himself.*

But my eyes had done a double take. *Wait. I see two small figures on the shore. One standing on a rock, jutting out into the water, the other standing close by on land. Skirts blowing toward the sea. Two dark haired women with their arms stretched out in front of them. Are they pleading for the man in the boat to save them? Or begging him to save himself and get to shore?*

My wife's voice had broken my concentration. I'd moved closer to her, to the painting. And the likeness I'd discovered from a distance had vanished and turned into thousands of blurred brushstrokes.

"I must have it," she'd said, and had put her hand to her chest. No artist's paintbrush could have captured the yearning in her eyes. And like her body might have crumbled, her hand had fallen to her side, and a tranquil smile had filled her face.

I bet she's imagining the perfect, happy ending.

Alex had embraced my arm. "It's expensive, Ty, but I'll keep it. Forever."

That's how long I'll love you. I'd handed Stephan a charge card, but I hadn't wanted the painting in our apartment. Why? I hadn't had a clue.

Chapter 17 - The Baby Shower
Sunday, June 11

Angela's due date according to her doctor had targeted the thirtieth of July. Her good friend, Tricia, from Los Angeles had taken two weeks of vacation to celebrate her dad's birthday and an early Father's Day. This had influenced the date set for the shower.

My daughter's knit maternity dress had stretched like the skin of a drum across her stomach. My son-in-law had helped her get situated in the overstuffed chair in our living room. And her bulky body had collapsed the cushion into a bowl-shaped crater. She'd folded her swollen hands in her lap. *She looks miserable. She's gained too much weight.*

I'd gotten our ottoman and propped her feet up. They'd hung over the sides of her flip flops. *Guess she couldn't get regular shoes on. Wish I could do something to make her more comfortable.* "It's time you stay home and rest," I'd said. "Tell Mrs. Schrader the doctor ordered you to."

"One of my pregnant coworkers asked for extra time off, and Mrs. Schrader fired her. She'd do the same to me."

"But you're her best graphic artist."

"Dad, the pay's good, and the travel time to work suits me. I want to keep my job."

Used to be my advice meant something.

"See you in about two and a half hours." Andrew had kissed Angela, and he'd turned to leave. I'd walked him to the door, and he'd turned to face me. "I've asked her to take a leave of absence from work, Ty. But she won't. And she gets upset. So, I stopped asking."

My wife had bustled into the living room with a covered plate. "Wait. Here's your lunch."

Our son-in-law had given Alex a hug. "Thanks."

"I'd better get back to the kitchen and finish prepping before guests start to arrive." Andrea's Pomeranian had yanked at his leash and caught her off guard. Our daughter had stumbled, but she had righted herself. "Call me Grace," she'd laughed. "Good thing you didn't expect me to take up dancing, Dad. Stop pulling, Spanky. Sorry, he'll settle down in a bit."

"Spanky's fine. All puppies like to explore," Angela had said.

"Yeah, he's cooped up in a kennel all day while Tom and I work."

I'm glad you brought him. He's adorable. And everyone's going to love him," Angela had said.

"Thanks. I won't let him interfere with the shower." Andrea had given her sister a kiss on the cheek and sat next to me on the couch.

I'd picked up Spanky and held him on my lap. "How's the drunk driver case coming along?"

Andrea had released a loud sigh, and the nail on her index finger had gone to the brown beauty mark above her left eyebrow. "Dad, I'm not at liberty to talk about any of my cases."

Huh. She talked to Alex about it on speakerphone. Better not say anymore. Guess she's stressed out. Sure hope she doesn't scrape that beauty mark off.

I'm certain I must have stared at Andrea's work in progress, and I had guessed I'd given myself away. She'd stopped picking, and her left hand had settled on her lap with her right.

Those slacks and blouse use to fit her. She's lost weight. Alex didn't want her helping with the baby shower, and now I understand why. She's nervous about that George Washington Bridge Case.

The doorbell had rung.

"Hi, I'm Tabby," a young woman with streaks of brown running through her blonde hair had said. "One of Angela's co-workers."

Besides the name and hair, something else about her had reminded me of a cat. "Hi, glad you could come. Follow me."

The woman had hugged my daughter then sat down on the loveseat. She'd placed her purse on the coffee table.

Our Lizzie, my son's wonderful wife, had shown up next, pushing a stroller with a big bow on it. Her mother, Karen, had carried in a large package.

More of Angela's co-workers from Schrader Graphic Designs, two secretaries and three fellow designers, had arrived, and Angela's friend, Tricia from college days, had followed close behind. Had she not introduced herself, I wouldn't have known our daughter's former classmate. Living in California had changed her. Her wrinkled, bronzed skin, and her short, juvenile dress, perhaps something she had designed, had sent mixed messages. She'd greeted Angela, still seated, with a hug and had said, "We need to catch up."

Angela had smiled, but not in her customary, all-out way. And the tone of her response, "For sure," had had a distinctive, cautious ring to it.

Alex had entered the living room holding a tray. "I hope everyone likes mimosas." She'd served the guests and handed Angela a glass. "Here's a low sugar orange juice for the mother-to-be." My wife had put the extra cocktails on the coffee table.

The doorbell had rung again. "Ty, the door, please," Alex had said, as if I hadn't known I was the designated doorman.

I hadn't met her before, but the hair had given her away. *Angela's boss, The Redhead.* Her spiked, red hair had jutted out like flames, and her large, silver hoop earrings had touched her blouse's collar. Not more than five feet tall, her green eyes had glared at me. "Mrs. Schrader, so glad you could make it. Follow me please."

"Do you mind," The Redhead had said, with no inflection she'd asked a question. She'd handed me a box wrapped in yellow paper. It had a huge green and yellow plaid bow with a silver baby spoon and fork fastened to its center.

Light as a feather.

I had escorted Angela's boss to the living room. My daughter had waved at her.

"Dear, I hope you don't intend to take six weeks off after delivery," Mrs. Schrader had said. She'd lowered herself to the couch and unbuttoned her suit jacket. The color had reminded me of a green apple. In a brusque, deep voice, "Sometimes women must make a difficult choice. Sometimes there's only one choice, if they value their job."

"Six isn't uncommon," Alex had spoken up. She'd handed Angela's boss a mimosa from the tray on the coffee table. "In fact, in New York--"

"Ah, the mother." The Redhead had scowled and turned toward Andrea. "And the identical twin. A lawyer, whose pockets fill from other people's anguish. Oh, well. We all must make a living somehow." Then what I'd guessed to be her attempt at a benevolent smile had appeared. Spanky had sniffed at her ankles. "What a cute Pomeranian."

Alex's pursed lips had sent me a message. The Redhead had ticked her off.

As if she'd remembered she should act like a gracious hostess, my wife had smiled. "It looks like everyone is here. Ladies, help yourselves to the lunch buffet on the island in the kitchen. Be sure to take a look at the cake before I cut it. I'll serve it while Angela opens her gifts."

My wife had turned to The Redhead and extended her hand. "May I help you up from the couch?"

The woman had frowned. "Dear, I'm quite capable of getting up by myself."

"How many children do you have . . . I'm sorry I don't know your first name."

"It's Miranda, Dear, but I prefer you address me as Mrs. Schrader." She had stared at Alex, as if she'd demanded her compliance. Silence had hung between the two women, like a rubber band stretched to its max. And my wife's tensed features had spoken volumes. *She's fuming.*

"To answer your question, I have no children. My job is my life." Her chin had tilted upward, and she'd made her way to the buffet line.

Angela and her guests had filed along the kitchen island to fill their plates, and I'd taken the role of photographer.

The guests had gone back to the living room to eat. But I, Alex, and our daughters had remained in the kitchen. Angela had held her cake, flanked by her mom and Andrea, and I had taken more pictures. After all, I had to get in on the action. I was going to be a grandpa again.

Our daughters had returned to the living room, but I'd stayed in the kitchen with Alex. We'd cut the cake and put it on serving trays. "I'm going to watch Angela open the baby's gifts," Alex had said.

"I want to watch, too."

"Okay, but please get the tray and serve the cake."

"All right." I had eyed two pieces of cake that hadn't fit on the tray. *I'll eat those later.*

"Open mine first, Angela. I have another obligation today," The Redhead had said as I'd entered the living room with the tray. "The yellow paper with the plaid green and yellow bow, Dear."

I'd begun distributing the cake, and my wife had picked up Mrs. Schrader's gift. The message her face had conveyed had forced me to stifle a laugh. *Yea, it's as light as a feather.* Alex had handed it to our daughter, whose forehead had wrinkled.

Angela had removed the fancy, silver baby spoon and fork and handed them to Andrea, who'd taken charge of the gift book.

That's my girl. No doesn't mean no to Andrea. Alex should have let her help plan the shower.

Angela had removed the yellow wrapping paper. I'd considered initiating a drum roll, but on second thought, I had reconsidered. *Better not. I'll catch it from all three of my raven-haired loved ones later.* Angela had removed a layer of green tissue paper and picked up an envelope that read: "For Baby Bartfield." She'd opened it and read the verse to herself. A check had emerged, and her eyes had widened in surprise. "What a generous gift. Thank you, Mrs. Schrader!"

Of course, I couldn't see the amount, but Alex, standing behind Angela, had, and she'd looked more taken aback than our daughter.

"You're my best graphic designer and a lovely young woman," Mrs. Schrader had said, and she'd smiled for the first time.

Shock had remained on Alex's face as she'd announced, "Everyone, please look at the bottom of your plate. If it has an X on it, raise your hand." My wife had handed a small, wrapped package to the winner, Tabby.

Mrs. Schrader had stood up and turned to face me. "I'm ready to leave. Escort me to the door."

Heat had risen up my neck. *I'm not one of your employees. Not that you should talk to them as if you own them, either.* Resentful, I'd done as she'd asked, and I'd opened the door for her, as well. She'd turned to face me. "Your daughters must have opposite personalities, Mr. Partridge. Am I right?"

I had hesitated. "Why would you ask that?"

"Lawyers must withstand a lot of pressure, right? Their job requires a strong backbone. Don't you agree, Mr. Partridge?" Mrs. Schrader's eyes had held steady, locked into mine. "Angela's twin is a lawyer, isn't she? Well, I guess I shouldn't compare your girls. But I'd say my employee doesn't work well under pressure."

This woman is really getting under my skin. Who does she think she is?

"I hope I haven't offended you."

Then why the smirk?

"Don't misunderstand. Angela's a wonderful girl. She's dedicated to her work. And she's an excellent designer. But she doesn't handle stressful situations well, like rushing to meet a deadline. I just wondered how your other daughter handles the taxing job she has."

I had taken her by the arm and had opened the door. "Let me help you down the steps, Mrs. Schrader. Wouldn't want you to fall." She'd pressed her cherry red lips together and mumbled something.

Old battle-axe.

Chapter 18 - Henry Gets the Boot
Monday, June 12

I'd eaten a stale chocolate donut from Rita's Bakery and had washed it down with my second cup of coffee. Alex's cell phone had rung. I hadn't heard the other side of the conversation, but her interspersed replies of "Oh my," and "That's hateful," teamed with her warrior's eyes, had told me it had something to do with one of our children.

She'd gotten off her phone, rinsed her coffee cup, and plunked down on a kitchen chair. A loud gust of air had burst through her pursed lips.

"Alex, what's wrong?"

"Mrs. Schrader called Angela last night. She ordered her to return to work in four weeks, instead of six. Otherwise, she's firing her."

"Can she demand that?"

"Angela isn't sure. She's going to ask Andrea."

The Redhead's a piece of work. "I hope Angela quits and finds a different job." I had put my arm around Alex. "Honey, we need to catch the train."

We'd entered The Silver Slipper and gone into the office. Alex had sat and put on her dance shoes. I'd given her a kiss and extended my hand. "Let me see if I can put a smile on your beautiful face. May I have this dance?"

Three men and four ladies had shown for our intermediate waltz class. I had partner with the extra lady. Alex had walked toward the CD player to start the music. Our students had needed a review of the previous lesson before learning new steps.

Henry Walsh had walked in, and he'd stood in the back of the room. Distracted, I'd excused myself and asked Alex to lead the fourth lady. *I can't believe he had the nerve to come back.*

I'd stood in front of him. His huge chest had heaved, like he'd just finished a marathon. And his clothes had reeked of smoke. *It's no wonder he can't breathe right.* "Leave," I'd said. "Ethan, who'd filled-in while Alex and I were gone, gave me a bad report about you. You've made advances toward Marie in our presence, too. *Leave*, you're no longer welcome here," I'd said.

"I'll behave, Ty. I promise."

"No, you're vulgar with the ladies. Get out!"

Alex had stopped dancing, approached me, and taken me aside. "Ty, you're making a spectacle of yourself. Let him dance with me, and after class we'll threaten to call the police if he shows up again. That'll scare him, and he'll stay away."

Henry had rejoined the class. The ladies had left him stand the odd man out. *They don't want to put up with his shenanigans. And Alex isn't, either. I'll teach him a lesson.* I'd grabbed his hand and forced him to face me in dance hold position. "I'm your partner today." One of the male students had roared with laughter, and others in the class had joined in.

Henry had tried to squirm free, but I'd tightened my grip. "The gentleman faces the lady and holds her right hand in his left at shoulder height, like so." I had yanked his arm up. This produces a graceful posture. And his right hand," here I'd made eye contact with Henry, "rests against her shoulder blade, like this." Henry's line of sight had shifted to the wooden floor, and he'd jerked his hand hard enough to free it from my grip. Then, he'd dug his fingers, into his doughy cheek, like a kid torturing a marshmallow. "Not funny, Ty."

I had taken his hand back into hold. He'd had two compression marks on his face, and his eyes, infused with anger, had darted from me to Alex and back.

"Gentlemen put your lady in closed hold. Henry, there aren't enough ladies. You'll continue practicing with me."

"No way four-eyes. Alex can dance with me."

If I had a belly like his, I wouldn't rub someone for wearing glasses.

"No. She's going to check the other students. I'm your partner."

"Ridiculous. And you and your wife address me as *Doctor* Walsh."

"Doctor? Of what?"

"Retired from veterinary medicine."

I'd faced him, grabbed his right hand with my left, and pushed our hands up to shoulder level. I'd placed my hand at his waist, as if he'd been the female. His rotund face had turned cherry red, and he'd broken free from me. "You won't have any further problems with a proper dance hold, will you Dr. Walsh?"

His eyes had turned watery, and the flabby fold of skin that hung from his chin had vibrated. He'd sighed, as if out of breath. But his eyes had hardened, and he had stared at me. *Old guy looks like he's itching to get revenge.*

I had taken my wife in closed dance hold. "Class, watch as Alex and I demonstrate the waltz promenade, done in six counts. I'll call out the man's steps. Ladies, your steps will be on the opposite foot and in the direction the man leads you. On count one, I step forward with my left foot. Counts two and three, I bring my right foot to my left, rotating both of our bodies in the diagonal direction we'll travel. For count four, I step through with my right foot. On count five, I bring my left forward and turn my body to face Alex. On count six, I slide my right foot up to meet my left. Watch Alex and I do a sequence of three promenades, counterclockwise around the ballroom." We'd demonstrated the steps, and I had instructed the men to take their lady in closed dance position. "I'll call out the man's steps and walk you through this sequence."

The bulbous sacks beneath Henry's eyes had pulsated. He'd held his hand out to Alex.

"No, Dr. Walsh. *I'm* your partner."

"I paid for this class, and I expect to dance with a woman."

I had turned my back to him. "Men, take your partner in closed dance hold and lead them in a sequence of three waltz promenades."

I'd kept an eye on Henry, who had stood off to the side.

"Let's move on." I'd taken Alex in hold. "Watch as we add on to the promenade. We'll start but not complete the third promenade. Instead of finishing counts five and six, I'll lead a lady's outside turn." I'd led two complete promenades, but on the third one, I'd brought Alex forward, lifted my left arm, and led her into an outside turn on counts one, two, and three. On step four I had continued forward. On step five I'd rotated back to face her, and I had brought my right foot to my left on count six.

Our students had performed the complete sequence three times and started clearing the ballroom.

I'd thought Henry had left. But in a gruff, loud voice he'd yelled from the doorway, "This isn't over. You're going to be sorry!"

Crazy old coot. "Get out and don't come back to this class or our swing class. You'll receive a refund check for both in the mail." He had sneered at me and left.

Alex and I had boarded the train exhausted from practicing for the performance at Adelphi. As luck had had it, we were able to sit instead of stand. I had wrapped my arm around her. She'd leaned her head against my shoulder and closed her eyes. The melody of her light breathing had played a sweet lullaby. *Wish I could describe how much I love you.*

But with mere minutes of sleep, Alex's phone had rung. Her head had shot up, and she'd reached in her purse to get it. "Hi Andrea." My wife's eyes had widened. "You're crying. What's wrong?" Alex's ear had remained pressed against the phone. "He'll come back."

"Who?" I'd said, but Alex hadn't answered. *Tom? Did they have a fight?*

"Okay, keep me posted. Love you, too. Bye."

"What's up?" I had said.

"Tom took Spanky outside to go to the bathroom."

I had breathed a sigh of relief.

"Andrea says he swore he hooked the dog's collar to the cable staked in the ground. The collar's a little big, though, and they think Spanky pulled his head out of it."

An awful thought had crossed my mind. *What if it's Commissioner Giovanni Fulcono's way of telling Andrea to back off?*

Chapter 19 - A Secret
Tuesday, June 16

Alex, Olivia, Ethan, and I had gone to the small kitchen on the second floor of The Silver Slipper for our lunch break. I'd chewed the first bite of my deli chicken sandwich, and my cell phone had rung. *Tom's number.* I had excused myself from the table and gone out to the hallway.

"Tom?"

"You're on lunch, right?"

"Yeah."

"Can you get away from Alex?"

"Already have. What's wrong?"

"Plenty. But first, this conversation can't get back to Andrea, or I'll catch it."

"It won't. You have my word."

"Since she took on the George Washington Bridge case things have happened, Ty. Dumped garbage, a punctured tire, and she swears a guy in a hat wearing sunglasses rides her bumper some mornings as she drives to work. She's received heavy breathing calls, but this morning, the caller spoke and made a verbal threat, 'Lose the case against Michael Fulcono or die.' Andrea described the caller's voice as sounding hoarse, husky. But she couldn't tell whether the caller was male or female."

Female? Mrs. Fulcono?

Tom's voice had quivered. "Now Spanky's missing. I told Andrea he slipped out of his collar, but I don't believe that. Not for a minute. He does his business and he's ready to get back inside. I shouldn't have lied to her, but he's like a third child to her. And our kids cried themselves to sleep last night. She's determined to get Michael Fulcono charged with vehicular manslaughter. She won't back down. She won't ask one of the men lawyers to handle the case. She won't. I've asked. She's my wife. My children's mother. What if one of our kids disappears? What if Andrea does?"

Seconds had passed. I'd heard his weighted breaths. "Tom, you okay?"

"Yeah. I shouldn't tell you this, but I'm scared, and I need to tell somebody. A witness read about the bicyclist's death in the *New York Daily News* and contacted the NYPD Legal Bureau. 'Driving fast and erratic,' is what the woman told Andrea. And she's going to testify at the trial. Michael Fulcono is as good as convicted. Andrea understands Commissioner Fulcono has political clout, and that he'll use his connections. He wants his son to get the lightest sentence possible. But my wife's determined to get a ruling of vehicular manslaughter in the first degree. And I don't think she's considered the repercussions to our family if she gets it. I'm afraid a hired thug will kill her or one of our kids. Don't tell Alex we had this conversation, and don't approach Andrea about what I've told you. The jagged pronunciation of his words had led me to a concrete conclusion--*He's crying.*

"I won't. But, keep me posted."

"Okay."

Andrea's in danger, someone took Spanky, and if enrollment doesn't increase, The Silver Slipper closes. Advertising a reduced rate for lessons has only brought us one new student. Dear Father in heaven help us.

Chapter 20 - Father's Day: Good News, Bad News
Sunday, June 18

After both daughters had married, Andrea and Angela had taken turns hosting a Father's Day get-together, but I'd decided I wanted to celebrate at our house that particular year. And I had canceled practice for that evening. Time spent with our adult children, grandkids, and son-in-laws, whom I'd loved like sons, had grown more precious. I had acknowledged mine and Alex's aging, the inevitability of death. But our daughter, Andrea, had put herself, her husband, and our grandchildren in harm's way. *I can't deal with one of them dying before us,* had gouged my mind.

Robert, and Lizzie had shown up at 11:30 with their three kids. Lizzie had handed Alex a bowl of potato salad. The twins, Marcus and Mindy, had taken a run at me. "Hi, Poppy!" As usual, I'd lifted both of them up, one in each arm. They'd given me and their nana hugs and kisses. Down on their feet again, they'd unpacked their bag of toys and begun to play. Eight-year-old Tyler had smiled and hugged Alex. He had greeted me with, "Hi Grandpa T. I brought my Super Soaker, like you asked me to."

Of course, I'd bought one, too. I'd told Alex it would keep him busy while the barbeque simmered in sauce. Lizzie had banned the twins from any water fight participation. And Alex had threatened to have my head if either of the five-year-olds had gotten blasted.

Robert had stood before Alex and me with a sober face and downcast eyes. "Mom and Dad, about using Adelphi University Dance Theatre for the performance. I-"

Alex's eyebrows had arched.

I had thought I'd prepared myself for disappointment, but I hadn't. My heart had sunk. "Thanks for trying, Son."

"I got the theatre! One Saturday night performance on July twenty-ninth!"

My wife's eyes had lit up, and she'd given Robert a one arm hug, as she'd balanced the bowl of potato salad with one hand. "Thank-you."

"Appreciate it, Son," I'd said and hugged him, too. *A performance at Adelphi will draw a larger audience than one at The Silver Slipper*, my inner voice had spoken. *I pray it draws clients to our studio.* A catch had lodged in my throat. *But if it doesn't? We can't keep operating in the red.*

Angela and Andrew had shown up, and we'd shared our good news. Both had congratulated us.

"Mom and Dad, we're having dinner with the Bartfields. We need to leave by 3:30."

"We understand," Alex had said. "I need to check on the baked beans and put this potato salad in the fridge."

She'll call Andrea.

Angela's swollen hands and feet, her slow gait, and her bulky body had caught my eye. *She looks miserable. And I bet Mrs. Schrader is grinding on her at work, too. Sure hope Angela has an easy delivery.*

Andrew had sat in a lawn chair and eyed my pork steaks.

I'd turned the steaks over, basted them with barbeque sauce. "I'm sure Andrea's family are on their way."

Tyler had filled both water backpacks for the Super Soakers. Antsy for his cousins, Sam, eleven, and tomboy Sarah, nine, to arrive, he'd strapped on his pack. "Grandpa T, let's start without them."

My grandson's patience had worn thin as he'd waited for me to stop conversing with his parents. He'd scuffed the toe of his tennis shoe into the lawn and dug out a clump of dirt.

Robert had noticed. "Tyler, Grandpa T doesn't want the little bit of grass he has destroyed. Take your soaker tank off, park your bottom on that lawn chair, and apologize."

He'd placed his water backpack on the ground, next to the lawn chair. "Sorry." Seated with his elbows propped on his knees, the palms of his hands had supported his head.

Black, thick hair like I used to have. And those downcast blue eyes, the same blue as mine. I had wanted to snatch him out of that chair and hug him. *Better not. Robert was right to correct him.*

Alex and Angela had brought out a pitcher of lemonade. Nana had liberated Tyler from his chair. The muscle in Robert's right cheek had tightened, and I had suppressed my desire to laugh. *I wouldn't have gotten away with that.*

I'd turned off the grill and left the lid down to keep the barbeque warm, right on target for my Father's Day meal, but Andrea, Tom, and the kids hadn't arrived.

"They call if they're running late," Alex had said, her forehead crumpled with lines. "Something's wrong."

"Honey. I told them we'd eat at 12:30." I had looked at my watch. "It's 12:55." A picture of Andrea at Angela's baby shower had revisited me. "She's run down from the trial, worried about Spanky, too."

"You're right," Alex had said. "Let's wait a little longer before we call. If she's not up to visiting, we can deliver food after we eat."

"Sounds good."

At 1:05, Andrea, Tom, and their twins, Sarah and Sam, had arrived. Our daughter's blotchy face, devoid of makeup, her puffy, red eyes, had gotten my attention. *Has something else happened?*

"Here, I picked these pies up yesterday at Rita's Bakery." Andrea's voice had peaked and plunged in rolling waves, and her right eye had had a twitch. "That young guy said his grandma's lemon meringue is the best. The other is chocolate, for the kids."

Alex had taken the pies from our daughter. "These look wonderful. But what's wrong?"

Our granddaughter had shrieked, "I want my puppy."

In a simultaneous motion, Andrea and Alex had reached for Sarah and cocooned her in embraces. Her outburst had ignited Sam. His jaw had tensed, and he'd shaken. His eyes had hardened into what I had labeled hatred, and he'd done an about-face. But the small, jerky vibrations from his shoulders had given his silent crying away.

Tom had put his hand on his son's shoulder. And the gravity of my eleven-year-old grandson's sorrow had pulled us all together. We'd formed a makeshift circle around the children. And my son-in-law had blown out a loud gust of air.

"No news about our dog. We're all a wreck," our daughter had said. Anger had emblazed her eyes. "Some piece of garbage took him. And he can't get loose to return home. That's what I think." Red blotches had formed on Andrea's neck.

"Will we ever see Spanky again?" Sarah's words had tumbled out between sobs.

Tom's mouth had twisted into tangled knots, "I don't know."

My son-in-law had made eye contact with me. "He was little, yeah, but that collar fit him, Ty. I picked it out myself. He *couldn't* have pulled out of it. I called the police last night. Reported him stolen. What else can I do?"

"You've done all you can, Andrew," I'd responded.

Andrea's beautiful but distorted face and the shiny blanket of pain on her eyes had chiseled away at me. And as I'd watched her cocoon Sam and Sarah in a protective sheath, I had made a decision. *Time to pay Commissioner Fulcono a visit. I'll make him tell me what he did with Spanky.*

Chapter 21- Spanky
Monday, June 19

Alex and I had gotten into our second week of a new session at The Silver Slipper. She hadn't complained about practices for *Dance of Cherry Blossoms* taxing her body. Neither had I. But stabbing calf pains and general fatigue had lashed out and reminded me of my age. On a nightly basis, I'd alternated ice packs with a heating pad, and I had taken ibuprofen for relief, also.

Olivia and Ethan in Ballroom Two had the beginner's contemporary class, and Alex and I had our beginner's foxtrot in Ballroom One.

"Last week's lesson consisted of the closed dance hold position and the basic step," I had reiterated. "I'm sure you remember; I altered the hold by asking the ladies and gentlemen to *not* have hip contact. This is meant to provide the ladies with a comfort zone. Watch while Alex and I review last week's lesson for the basic foxtrot step." I'd put on a CD, and my wife and I had danced counterclockwise around the ballroom.

I'd stopped the music. "Gentlemen, take a partner, and put her in the altered closed dance position. Alex and I will check your framing, dance hold, and basic step. If everything is good, we'll move on."

I'd stopped the CD. "Looks good. Watch as Alex and I do one basic step and add a sway step." I had taken my wife in dance hold. "Gentlemen, here's our basic. Now, with my left foot, I'll step left and to the side, and brush my right foot to meet my left." Alex, of course, followed my lead, using her right foot to step to the side, and she'd brushed her left to meet her right. "Next, we take a side-together, side-together step, like so, and it brings us back into position to perform a basic step, another sway step, or a different step. Men find a partner, and we'll try this."

All the students, as I'd expected, had performed the easy sway step correctly. "Let's move on to the corner step," I'd said. "This will also add variety to the basic step, and it helps prevent bumping into another couple on the dance floor. Watch while Alex and I demonstrate. I'll call out the man's steps. I walk forward with my left foot, rock back on my right, replace the weight to my left, and turn my lady and myself with a quarter turn. Next, I draw my left foot back to my right. I can continue leading another corner turn and another, like so, and if I wish to, I can lead Alex on to complete a full circle."

We'd eaten a light dinner. I'd gone into the living room, sat on the loveseat, and propped my feet up on the coffee table. *I'm exhausted. I don't want to practice tonight. No. I do. The performance must be a success, or we won't draw new students to The Silver Slipper.*

A stabbing pain had shot up the back of my left calf. I had drawn it up toward my trunk, rubbed it until I'd gotten relief. *Forget the ice and heat. What's the use?*

Drowsy, I had allowed myself to relax, and my head had dropped back on top of the upright cushion. I had decided to close my eyes and catch a few winks, but my line of sight had landed on the painting. *Out of all the paintings at that gallery, why'd she want this one? I don't like it. The guy's battling a bad storm. In real life he wouldn't make it to shore, but Alex, my sweet optimist, with her happy endings, must have believed he would. One of the reasons I love you.*

My wife had approached me; her lips had caressed my cheek. "Time to leave for practice. I'll get our dance shoes." She'd turned and walked down the hall and entered our bedroom.

"Okay, Honey." I'd gotten up from the couch, and my cell phone had rung. "Hello."

"Ty, Spanky's dead." Tom had said.

"What? How are the kids?"

"They still think he's well cared for and loved."

"Good. So the police found him?"

"No, Andrea did, after work. A picture of an arrow, pointing down, dangled from the car's door handle on the driver's side. She crouched down, looked under the car, and saw Spanky's bloody body."

"The guy who did it has some nerve," I'd said. "That's a busy street. Piece of garbage must not have worried about getting caught.

"I got there as quick as I could," Andrew had said. "The police officer pulled our little dog's bloody, stiff body out from under the car.

He had gashes all over him. Andrea screamed four letter words and bawled at the same time. I couldn't console her. I picked up sleeping pills from the pharmacy and convinced her to get in bed. She fell asleep about twenty minutes ago. The kids think she has the flu. I had to keep them away from her. No way could I let them see Andrea. Not in the shape she'd been in."

She thought of Spanky as a third kid. My face, my neck, my whole body had heated up, like a furnace. I'd wished for ten minutes alone with Spanky's killer.

"I gotta go. I need to check on Andrea."

Why would anyone kill that sweet, little dog? Mutilate it? They're either crazy or desperate. Maybe both. Commissioner, did you do it? Or did you pay someone to do it? Andrea won't throw the case. So is she next?

Chapter 22 - Delivery Time
Saturday, June 24

The landline phone had rung. I'd rolled onto my side and squinted at the LED alarm clock on the nightstand. The numbers, 4:57, had jumped out at me.

Alex had rolled onto her back.

"Don't get up. I've got it." My hands had pushed against the mattress. I had thrust myself up, swung my legs over the side of the bed, and grabbed the receiver off of its cradle. *I'm going to give them a piece of my mind.*

"Hello," I'd said. My wife's breath had tickled the side of my neck.

A muffled mix of voices had transmitted into my ear. And if someone had intended to give me a message, I hadn't weeded it out. "What? Who is this?" I'd said.

The New Jersey voice that Alex and I hadn't possessed had blurted through the receiver, "We're at Lenox Hospital."

"Andrew?"

"Sorry for not responding at first, Ty. Dr. Radovich came in the room. I wanted to hear what she had to say. Angela should deliver within the hour. She asked me to call you."

Alex and I had thrown on clothes and caught the train.

Andrew had stood next to Angela's bed in the delivery room. He'd held her hand and acted as her breathing coach. And my son-in-law's acts of devotion had won my admiration.

Alex and I had kissed Angela's forehead. Not in a receptive mood, she'd said, "Don't hover. Don't talk." And with that coming from our easygoing daughter, I'd backed up.

"Okay, Honey," Alex had said, "I understand."

"It's not just the contractions," our son-in-law had said and winced as though he'd just had one. "Dr. Radovich told Angela she needs to deliver now. We're having a C-section."

"*I'm* having a C-section, Andrew."

A chill had run down my spine. The falling plate in our kitchen had replayed in slow motion. The tapered point, like the blade of a knife, had again rung true. First Hannah, next Spanky, and now Angela. One of my mom's old sayings had come to mind, "Bad things come in threes." *At least I can rest at ease. The omens' predictions are fulfilled.*

My son-in-law's eyes had focused on the floor. "She didn't want... neither of us wanted it to go this way. But Dr. Radovich says the possibility of eclampsia has forced an early delivery."

"Eclampsia? What's that?" Alex had blurted out.

"When high blood pressure causes seizures," Andrew had said. "Angela's gained too much weight. Her hands, feet, and face are swollen, and she's vomited the last few days. She made me promise not to tell you. Waiting for nature to take its course, she could have a seizure."

She had swollen feet at her shower. And Father's Day she didn't look well.

A nurse had checked Angela's temperature, pulse, and blood pressure, then she'd examined the IV bag. "She's been given something to help her relax. She's prepped and ready to go. The C-section takes about fifteen minutes, then delivery of the placenta and suturing, another forty-five. We'll take good care of her. Mr. Bartfield can go to the operating room with her, but the rest of you must go to the waiting room. When she's back in her room, someone will let you know."

Bed rest. That's what she needed. Instead, she sat at a computer all day. I'd turned to Alex. "We'd better call the rest of the family and tell them Angela's having surgery." I had glanced at the clock on the wall. "It's not quite six."

"Lizzie's up," Alex had said. "She grocery shops early Saturday mornings, while Robert's home with the kids. And I would bet Andrea's up working on that bridge case. I'll call both of them."

"Honey you're upset. I'll do it. Close your eyes. Try to relax."

I'd stood under the blue canopy. A light breeze had tickled my face. *After I tell Andrea about her sister's C-section, I'll ask about her progress with the GWB case.*

A prickly, "Dad, what's up?"

I had disregarded her barbed words. "Angela's at Lenox Hospital."

A breathy, "Oh. But she isn't due yet."

"Her blood pressure is elevated, and she's having a C-section. She and the baby are in good hands with Dr. Radovich," I'd said, though I wouldn't have said it when I'd first met the young doctor. *I'm not mentioning the eclampsia. Or the case. Andrea is stressed-out enough.*

"I'll be there in twenty minutes. And sorry I sounded cranky, Dad."

She has her hands full with the bridge case. "It's best if you visit your sister tomorrow. Angela needs to remain quiet and sleep today." *I bet Andrea's blood pressure is up, too.* "I wish you had another attorney helping with the bridge case." *No. I wish she had handed the case off to another attorney.*

"Okay, tell her I'll visit tomorrow. But keep me posted. And I can handle the case by myself. I'm as good or better than any attorney that works with the police department."

"I didn't mean to suggest otherwise, but Spanky's death has made this case personal."

"You're right. The scumbag sent me a message to back off. No way. I'm going to get a conviction. But I've run into a problem. The woman who witnessed Michael Fulcono's car hitting David Bowman backed out of testifying. She's saying the accident happened fast, and she isn't sure what she saw. Who do you think got her to change her story?"

Lots of stress in her voice. And she divulged another fact about her case.

"I'd bet money on Commissioner Fulcono, Dad. Text me later, after Angela's out of surgery. Tell my sister I love her."

Yeah, if he butchered Spanky, he'd have no problem harassing a witness.

I had called Robert and our daughter-in-law, Lizzie. They'd wanted to visit Angela, too. But I'd persuaded them to wait, also. *Better not tell them about the eclampsia, either. I didn't tell Andrea.*

Andrew's pale face and sheepish smile had greeted me as I'd entered the waiting room. My eyes had flitted to my wife. Her head shake had cued me in.

"Why aren't you with Angela?" I'd said.

"Dr. Radovich started to cut Angela's stomach open, and I got sick," Andrew had said. His right leg had shaken in sporadic bouts.

I had sat next to Alex and remained quiet. *Poor guy. But I wish he'd stop that.*

One after the other, families had gotten notified they could see their loved ones. I'd checked the wall clock for the umpteenth time. The nurse told us the C-section would take an hour. An hour and thirty minutes had passed. I had loosened Alex's grip from my sweaty arm. "I'm going to ask the receptionist why we haven't heard anything yet."

"No. I'll do it," Andrew had said.

Our son-in-law had returned. He'd flopped down in the chair on the other side of Alex. In a tone seasoned with dread, "The receptionist said she'll check." His bowed torso and bent head had depicted a surrender to stress.

Alex had rested her head on my shoulder, and her body had folded into me. Her somber, downcast eyes had taken me down memory lane. I shouldn't have let her give dance lessons when she was pregnant. But she had wanted to.

I'd pictured my wife entering our ballroom with tears streaming down her eyes. "I'm bleeding," she'd said. Those two words had flung me into action. I'd sent the students home, called a cab and the hospital. Our situation had turned out well. The doctor had stopped the bleeding, and Alex had delivered earlier than expected. But she and Robert were fine.

Why didn't Angela's doctor put her on bed rest? I bet she did, but that boss of hers threatened to fire her. What if Angela and our grandchild aren't fine? If she loses this baby, it's The Redhead's fault.

Thirteen minutes had passed. The receptionist had come out to the waiting room. "All three of you can see Angela, but please keep your visit brief."

We'd followed Andrew. Dr. Radovich had caught us before we'd entered Angela's room. The doctor's slouched stance had communicated exhaustion. "Angela and your daughter are fine, Mr. Bartfield."

With this news Alex's face had beamed. "A girl! I was right!"

Dr. Radovich had turned to Andrew, and I'd taken in the varnish pooling in her eyes. "I'm sorry, the boy didn't make."

Alex and I had locked eyes. "Boy?" my wife had whispered. She'd clung to me, trembled in my arms, and a river of tears had run down her cheeks. She had turned to Andrew. "Why didn't you tell us there were two?"

"I thought we should, but Angela wanted to surprise you."

"That's why she gained so much weight," Alex had said. I'd made eye contact with her and nodded, and she'd acknowledged my unspoken request to let it rest.

"Can we see her?" My wife had said.

"She's experiencing gas pains, but that's common after a C-section," Dr. Radovich had said. "The anesthesia has worn off, and her incision site is sore. The pain medication hasn't kicked in, and I've told the nurse to allow only a brief visit. Angela needs to rest."

"How many days will my wife remain in the hospital?"

"If her discharge flow is normal and I'm confident about her strength, I'll release her in three or four days. But she'll need to take it easy for four to six weeks. Any other questions, Mr. Bartfield?"

"No. And thank you, doctor."

"Your daughter's beautiful," Dr. Radovich had said.

"Thank you. Her name's Abigail Grace. We'll call her Abbey."

The doctor had smiled. "Abbey's in the nursery waiting to meet you."

Andrew had kissed Angela and told her he loved her. We had done the same.

Our daughter's eyes had glazed. "Mom. Dad. I lost the little boy."

"Dr. Radovich told us," I'd said.

Alex had bent over and kissed Angela's forehead. "We love you. Thank-you for giving us a beautiful granddaughter. We're so happy you and Abigail Grace are okay. But now you need to rest."

"I am tired. Andrew, please take my parents to the nursery."

Our daughter's eyes had fluttered. *Sleep well*, I'd thought. *She's exhausted. She went under the knife, but she's alive. Thank-you, God.*

Our son-in-law had tapped on the window and mouthed, "Bartfield." A nurse had picked up our granddaughter and presented her at the window. This grandpa's pride had swollen. *Doe-eyes, rosy cheeks, and a head full of black hair. Reminds me of our newborn twins.*

Tears had rolled down my wife's cheeks.

"She's perfect," Alex had said. I'd put my arm around my wife. And like a tug of war, my heart had experienced both elation and sadness. And I'd expected Alex's had, too. In the quiet of my mind, I'd thanked God for keeping my daughter safe, for giving us a granddaughter. And I'd prayed for my deceased grandson, who'd gone to heaven.

I had taken Alex by the hand to leave the hospital. And a voice inside my head had whispered, *Are the omens satisfied, yet?*

Chapter 23 - The Informant
Monday, June 26

Our day had finished at The Silver Slipper. I'd grabbed my thermos from my office desk and chugged a cup of coffee to get caffeinated for two hours of practice with our dance troupe. I'd wanted my body and mind energized, sharp. Alex had started distributing deli sandwiches we'd had delivered.

With our stage performance for *Dance of Cherry Blossoms* set for the following month, Robert's fine-tuned critical remarks at practices had had me beaming with pride. I'd had no doubts about the choreography or our son's recruitment of talented Adelphi students and staff. But two questions had lingered in my mind. *Will the performance draw new students to The Silver Slipper? And if it does, will it draw enough to keep our business open?*

  About to exit the office, the phone had rung. "Hello." I'd listened, waited for a response.

  A labored exhale had come through the receiver. "Is this Ty Partridge?"

  "Yes. Who is this?"

  "Shut up and listen. The person threatening to harm your daughter is insane. And I mean, at one time committed to a psychiatric facility. The lawyer better lose, or she'll die." Click.

  "Hello!" *Gruff, raspy voice. Sounded forced, though.* Tom's description of Spanky found ripped open had flashed through my mind.

  Alex had entered the office. "Robert and some of the dancers have arrived."

  "Honey, someone called the office phone a few minutes ago. I'm sure they disguised their voice. They told me that if Michael Fulcono is charged with vehicular manslaughter, Andrea dies."

A surge of tears had run down my wife's cheeks. "I can't practice tonight, Ty."

"Me either. I'll tell Robert."

Our son hadn't asked why. He'd understood what the performance at Adelphi had meant for Alex's and my future. He'd understood something of huge importance had prompted his mother and me to leave.

Alex had sat next to me on the couch. "I'm calling Andrea. She has to give the bicyclist's case to another prosecutor in the DA's Vehicular Crime Unit."

"Tom's tried to convince her to do that. She won't. Nobody and nothing will make her hand it off, Honey."

As if a light bulb had illuminated my wife's understanding of the situation, her face had tightened. "Spanky's death is connected to the GWB case, isn't it?"

"I think so."

"Oh, Dear God," Alex had said. She'd hurried down the hallway, and her shoulder had bumped against the painting she'd bought in SoHo. Her valued piece of art had hung lopsided.

I'm glad it didn't fall. She doesn't need anything else upsetting her.

She'd entered our bedroom and closed the door.

I hope she can relax and sleep.

The tilted angle of the picture had drawn my attention. The two women on shore and the man in the boat had looked as if they'd fall into the water. A strange sense of unfinished business about the artist's story and how it played out had sparked my imagination.

I'd gotten up to straightened it. With it righted, I had again examined it. *What does this painting portray? The outstretched arms of the women on shore reach out toward the sea, toward the man in the boat. But why? For their rescue? For their father's? Or one of the women's lovers?*

The artist's brushstrokes breathe life onto the canvas. There's a story. But what is it? And how does it end? Happy? Sad? The outcome had eluded me, as it had at the art gallery.

The momentary distraction hadn't lessened my distress about Andrea's safety. *I don't want to wake Alex, if by chance she's fallen asleep. It's the couch for me tonight.*

A draft across my body had awakened me. The spirits of Reverend Maynard and my sister had stood next to the couch. "I'm glad to see you," I'd whispered. But my further observation had sobered me. Two wavy rivers of tears had flowed down Allison's cheeks, and the reverend's gloomy, wrinkled face had given off a vibe of hopelessness.

"What's wrong, Allison?" She'd turned to the reverend, as if she'd needed his approval to speak.

The reverend had scratched his white goatee. "Go ahead, tell him."

"You've not understood the prophetic signs, Brother. Your human nature doesn't grasp the whole truth of their meaning. Or from whom these messages have come. Cancel the performance. Please."

Chapter 24 - Trouble Returns
Friday, June 30

Engaged in teaching a modern dance move, Alex and I hadn't observed an intruder who'd entered the ballroom.

"You owe me dance lessons!"

I hadn't needed to turn around to verify who had shouted. His gruff voice had announced trouble had arrived. *The old, irritating pervert is back.* I'd turned around to face him. "Henry get out."

He had ignored my demand, and his bulbous eyes had born into me. I had disregarded his snide stare down with all the self-control I'd been able to manage. "Leave. Now. Or I'll call the police."

He'd continued to glare at me, and his bottom lip had stuck out. "I'm not afraid of you."

"Why are you here? You didn't enroll in modern dance. And I refunded you for the two classes you registered for."

"I don't want the refunds." He'd reached in his pocket. He'd thrown the check, and it had glided to the floor.

Alex had left our students practicing the new move we'd taught, and she'd joined me. "Pick up the check and leave, Henry. Or I'll call the police."

His face had reddened, and he'd moved closer to us. "No. I . . . wa, want to attend the waltz and swing classes. A coughing fit had erupted, and a high-pitched whistling had escaped. And his eyes had turned wild with anger or panic, I hadn't decided which. His frenzied hand had rummaged through his pants pocket.

Does he have a gun? I had gotten in position, readied myself to grab it from Henry. But he'd pulled out an inhaler instead. And as though his life had depended upon it, he'd shook it, tilted his head back, and inserted it into his mouth. He'd driven down the top of the canister, pumped it twice, and inhaled slow and deep while he'd held his breath. He'd blown out a big gust of air through his mouth, and the panic in his eyes had disappeared.

"Asthma," Henry had said.

Alex had picked up the check and had handed it to him. "We're sorry you have health problems. But I'm calling the police if you don't leave." She had turned and made her way back to our students.

I had taken hold of his arm, helped him to the door. "Here's your check," I'd said. And I had put it in his shirt pocket.

He'd pulled it out, thrown it on the floor. "Shove it!" Henry had turned and mumbled something before he'd exited.

Did he say, "You'll be sorry?"

Chapter 25 - The Cherry Blossom Tree
Wednesday, July 12

Robert and his dancers from Adelphi University had arrived. Our dancers from The Silver Slipper had already warmed up in Ballroom One. But I'd gone into panic mode. *How's it all going to come together? Our performance is two-and-a-half weeks away. And if our one-night stand doesn't turn out spectacular, I haven't got a prayer's chance of saving this studio.*

Minutes later, my son's colleague, Brandon, had entered ballroom one with a large box. He'd sat it on the floor and walked over to us. "The design students finished the costumes. I think you're going to be pleased."

"Dancers continue practicing in your assigned age-groups," I'd said. "Come on Robert and Alex, let's take a look."

One by one, Brandon had removed the various costumes for us to examine. The students' designs had differentiated the various groups of the Japanese cherry blossoms dead-on.

"Hand them out tonight, Ty, and have everyone try them on," Brandon had said. "If any need alteration, I'll have the students fix them right away, and I'll get them back to you Friday."

"You got those done fast, buddy," Robert had said. "And they look great. I had no doubt about the workmanship you'd require from your students. Thanks for all your help."

"Yeah, thank-you," I had said. "Without you, we couldn't have gotten everything organized fast enough."

"Fast enough for what, Ty?" My wife had said.

My son had motioned to Brandon. "I have a few questions about the stage lighting. Let's talk over here." I had witnessed my son's slick maneuver to remove his colleague from the discussion Alex and I had needed to have.

"What's up?"

"Honey, I've had to get into our savings to pay the bills. Sorry. I should have told you."

Alex's stunned reaction had guilted me. "Are you angry?"

"No. I get it. You didn't want me to worry, and I love for that. But I'm upset with myself. I shouldn't have bought that expensive painting. I'll return it."

"Don't. You love it, and you're keeping it. I've contacted smaller, local dance studios. Co-owners of one acted interested in buying The Silver Slipper. They want more space. And they think most of their students would follow them. I believe most of our current students would remain. If we have to sell the studio, the new owners should have a profitable business."

Tears had welled up in Alex's eyes. Unaware that Robert had returned to get us for practice, he had heard at least part of our conversation. "Mom and Dad, don't sell. I'd bet money our performance brings new students to The Silver Slipper. I've advertised *Dance of Cherry Blossoms* everywhere I could. Wait. Please. I believe we can save the studio."

Alex had forced what I'd labeled a weak smile. "We appreciate all your effort, Son. I hope you're right."

The three of us had returned to the rest of the dance troupe, and Brandon had approached us. "Thank you," I'd stuck out my hand.

"You're welcome, Ty. Robert told me what's at stake if the performance doesn't bring more students to your studio. And he's told me what The Silver Slipper means to him. He's my best friend." Brandon had patted Robert on the back. "I'll do everything in my power to help him, help you."

"Alex had run her hand across the petals on her costume. "These are beautiful."

A smile had lit up Brandon's face. "I'll have Michaela Caplan's kimono by Tuesday," he'd said. "Does Tyler have his lines memorized?"

Don't worry about my grandson, I'd thought. He's a chip off the old block.

"Yes, he does," Robert had said. "And I've worked on voice inflection and acting with him. Lizzie helped me pick out a pair of shorts and T-shirt for his costume. And tomorrow night, we'll have a full cast."

"Wonderful," Brandon had said. "I can't wait for Tyler to meet Michaela. She has the nurturing personality of a grandmother. He'll like her."

Robert had looked at his watch. "I couldn't get permission to assemble our prop in Adelphi's Dance Theatre this soon, Dad. But we need to implement it for the rest of our rehearsals. Some guys are due to deliver it here any minute. I'll need help getting the tree pieces inside. We're assembling it tonight. Surprised?"

"Not a bit, Robert. No obstacle has held you back yet."

"Matt, Dave, Brian, follow Robert," I'd said. "Alex, will you take charge of the girls and critique their movements? Tomorrow's practice we'll work on perfecting their performance on the tree limbs."

She had smiled. "That'll be interesting."

Two trucks with Bruckman Steel written on the side had pulled up. We'd approached the first one. Robert had introduced us to his buddy, Jake, who'd borrowed his dad's trucks for hauling. *Hope I don't rupture my gut*, had entered my mind.

Jake had climbed into the bed of the truck and slid the bottom of the tree trunk forward. Dave, Brian, and I had lifted it without much effort, and we'd carried it toward the front entrance of The Silver Slipper.

"Wow. It's light. But looks realistic," I'd said.

"The frame's made of metal alloy," Robert had said. "It has a high strength-to-weight ratio. And there are trusses, too. It's sturdy, Dad."

"Good. Looks great, too, Robert."

"The art students at Adelphi put layers and layers of plaster over the wire wrapped newspaper around the framework. After the sculpting dried, they painted the tree, blending colors together to make it look realistic."

We'd carried the frame and had deposited it along the back wall of Ballroom One. Well, *at least it won't interfere with dance lessons, there.*

Jake and his helpers had unloaded the second truck. They'd carried in the branches, truss supports, and platforms for footholds. Robert, me, and our other three male dancers had assembled the tree. Alex had kept the rest of the dance troupe practicing.

Relief had washed over me. *Still enough floor space to accommodate classes*, had danced through my mind. *Thank-you, God. Alex and I need the income.*

Chapter 26 - A Full Cast
Thursday, July 13

Now that our main stage prop, the Japanese cherry blossom tree, had gotten assembled, the movements we'd practiced on the floor had needed fine-tuning. Dancing for the first time on our assigned foothold platform, I'd had concerns about precision and gracefulness. I'd understood I needed my undivided concentration to perform the ballet and modern dance movements on the much smaller platform. *Don't mess up*, had looped nonstop through my head.

Robert had reassured me Michaela Caplan, his colleague from Adelphi University, and Tyler had had their lines memorized, and they'd do fine at their first practice. Family and work-related obligations had made it impossible for Michaela to participate in previous practices. And without her present, Robert hadn't wanted his son to work with a fill-in. He'd told me building rapport with a performer, then switching to another, wouldn't have worked well with an eight-year-old.

I'd had confidence in Robert's words and believed what he'd said. But a vision of my grandson chasing me with his water gun had played in my mind. I had wanted Tyler to play the magomusuko in *Dance of Cherry Blossoms*, but I hadn't imagined how we'd keep my grandson on task.

My son had positioned me and Alex on branches in the center of the tree. The paired buds had had branches near one another, and they'd made a configuration around us.

Silk flowers sewn on the costumes' hoods had varied in color and size. These, as well as the tights, in diverse shades of green, had differentiated the age groups.

My son had assured the dance troupe of the tree's strength to support our bodies. He'd noted the additional braces, painted to blend with the tree's trunk, along with the attached footholds, which afforded stability. He'd reassured the ladies of their safety, and everyone had mounted their foothold.

Robert had directed Michaela, playing the part of the grandmother, and Tyler, playing the role of her grandson, to sit on their prop, the park bench, set at an angle. This had put them in view of the Japanese cherry blossom tree. And it had also allowed for audience observation of their actions.

"I have a few announcements before we start practice," Robert had said. He'd pointed toward the park bench. "This is Michaela Caplan, Associate Professor in Adelphi's Theatre Department. She's portraying the Japanese sobo. And this young man, Tyler, my son, will play the role of her magomusuko. Please welcome them to their first rehearsal."

The troupes' applause had echoed in The Silver Slipper. But nerves had had my stomach rolling. *Tyler, please remember your lines.*

"I have one more bit of business before we start practicing," Robert had said. "Students from Adelphi's Music Department, Mellissa Comstock and Josh Purcell, spliced instrumental music together for the CD we're using. Though they aren't present, I want to have them recognized for their amazing work. Let's give them a round of applause." Again, applause echoed. "Thank-you for acknowledging their contribution.

"Now, I'd like to take a few minutes to emphasize the importance of touching the audience emotionally. Music depicts mood, like dance does. If it's ominous, it cultivates a sense of danger and tension. Then the flowers' fast, erratic movements must show fear, anxiety. When the music softens, it depicts a tender or sad moment, and your movements must portray contentment or sorrow. Dance troupe, your job is to *humanize* the cherry blossoms. Any questions?" Robert had paused. "Dad, Mom, anything to add?"

Alex and I had shaken our heads no. "Everyone take your places," I'd said. "Scene One, *The Newborns.*" Robert had started the CD, and whimsical music had played.

Costumed in the kimono Brandon had designed for her, Michaela's husky voice had delivered her lines with a slight quiver. And she'd impersonated an elderly Japanese sobo with perfection.

My grandson, Tyler, had kept his lines straight, and his body language had mimicked that of a young boy's. Costumed in shorts, a T-shirt, and tennis shoes, he'd looked like the typical kid. *He did great. Pulled off the role of the magomusuko like a pro.*

I'd watched the two dancers, Kami and Brian. They had performed their parts as cherry blossom buds well, also. I had envisioned my son and daughters as newborns, long ago, and a lump had formed in my throat. *The audience will love the story our performance tells.*

We'd completed the first scene, and Robert had asked for my opinion. "Anything you'd like changed, Dad?"

"Not a thing, Son. I loved it."

"Really? You look worried."

"I'm not. You've done a great job organizing and critiquing. Without your painstaking efforts, the performance wouldn't have been possible. Thank-you for your tireless energy. I guess my age has caught up with me, Robert." But I had lied. Inside my brain a clock had ticked, and it had marked off time. And besides the pressure to succeed at saving the dance studio, a more important goal had owned my thoughts.

"Take it easy the rest of the practice, Dad."

My eldest had directed the next two scenes, and pride swelled inside me. He had created a work of art. *The performance may draw more students to The Silver Slipper. And God, I'm praying it does. But God, please, please show me a way to keep Andrea alive.*

Everyone else had left. Alex and I had stopped in the office to change into our street shoes. The phone had rung. *Someone must think we give evening classes.* "Hello. This is-"

"What? Slow down Tom."

Alex eyes had widened, and she'd drawn in a deep breath. "What's wrong?"

I had finished listening to my son-in-law and hung up. "Someone called Andrea and threatened to kill her."

Chapter 27 - Ty's Decision
Friday, July 14

Stressed-out from Tom's phone call and exhausted from practice, we'd caught the train, our destination home. Alex had rested her head on my shoulder, snuggled her body close to mine. Her ashen face, downcast eyes, and silence had sent a message. *Bet she's thinking about Andrea's safety, too.* I had enveloped my wife's right hand in my hands. My touch hadn't caused a full-blown cry, but her eyes had leaked tears onto my shirt.

Mere minutes had passed, and she'd raised her head. Her hand had jerked away from me, and she'd laced her fingers in a white-knuckled death grip on her lap.

"You're thinking about the threat to Andrea's life, aren't you, Honey?" What-ifs had unnerved me, too. I'd envisioned Spanky's mutilated body. *Any guy who'd do that is crazy. He won't think twice about killing Andrea.*

Alex hadn't replied, but her glassy eyes had spoken.

"It's on my mind, too. The commissioner thinks he'll scare her, and she'll throw the case. But we both know she won't. I'll make him stop tormenting her."

How? By confronting him? What if he decides to kill you? What if I end up burying a husband and daughter?"

"I'll be careful. I promise."

"But if he killed Spanky . . . " Alex's voice had faded away, and her white-knuckled hands had parted. She'd broken away from my embrace. "I love you, Ty. You're a wonderful husband and father. And I'm as worried about Andrea's safety as you are. I want to protect her. But the right way. She's not a little girl. She's a woman. An extremely independent one. If you confront Giovanni Fulcono and she finds out, you'll insult her. Contact the police instead. They've dealt with situations like this before. They have a report on file about Spanky. Tell them about the call. An undercover officer could follow her and keep her safe."

"This isn't a movie. First, there's no proof the commissioner killed Andrea and Tom's dog. There's no proof he threatened to kill Andrea on the phone, either. She doesn't need to know everything I do, Honey. She won't find out."

My wife's forehead had wrinkled, her raised eyebrows had arched. She'd locked eyes with me. "I can't talk you out of this?"

"No."

"Then tell me what you intend to do."

"Talk to him. Get the drift if he's capable of doing what was done to Spanky. If I'm convinced he is, I'll go to the police and ask them to assign a plain clothes officer to keep an eye on Andrea."

"If they won't? Then what's going to happen, Ty?"

I hadn't responded but etched in my brain I'd had a plan.

We'd entered our apartment, and a cascade of tears had streamed down Alex's face. "You're going to confront Commissioner Fulcono, aren't you? If our daughter ends up dead, I won't forgive you." She had done an about-face, and I'd heard the bedroom door slam.

I hope she can rest. I'd sat at my office desk and pulled up the phone number for The New York /New Jersey Port Authority. My fictitious name and fabricated story had gotten me an appointment with Commissioner Fulcono.

He thinks scare tactics will force Andrea to throw the trial. But it won't. She's proud of her work. And stubborn. See you Monday afternoon, Fulcono. I hope you'll come around and leave my daughter alone. But if you don't, I'll convince you to.

Chapter 28 - Enlightenment
Saturday, July 15

Five minutes into ballet class, Henry had entered Ballroom One. Alex had done a double take, as if she hadn't believed her eyes. "What's he want? He isn't registered for this class."

"Keep them practicing the pirouette. I'll take care of him." I'd taken Henry by the arm, turned him around. "Let's talk in the hall." He'd sneered, and his nose had flared in and out, like a bull ready to charge, but he'd followed me out of the ballroom.

His bottom lip had buckled, and he'd looked like an old, overweight bully. "Guess you're afraid of a scene in front of your students, huh?"

"I don't like my classes disturbed, if that's what you mean. Why are you here?"

"I'm suing you for slandering my character. And my lawyer says I'll win. Ha, ha. How do you like them apples? The big payout is gonna force you and Alex into bankruptcy. You'll have to sell your studio to pay me." Henry's malicious laugh had prefaced another threat. "Or I'll *own* The Silver Slipper, and you'll work for me. Yeah, I'd like that better."

You old fool. The studio is operating in the red. And you're crazy if you believe I'd work for you. "First of all, I didn't slander you. I corrected you. You placed your hands on a female in an inappropriate way during swing class. So, I banned you from swing and waltz class, too. You received full refunds for both. And I didn't have to give them to you."

The dramatic, upward tilt of Henry's chin had displayed his arrogance. "Didn't understand your directions, Ty."

That's a bunch of crap. "You understood, but you chose not to follow them. Tell you what, have your lawyer send me a copy of the charges. I'll have my lawyer get back to him with a list of women from swing class who'd jump at the chance to testify against you. Heck, they might decide to sue you."

Henry had squeezed his eyes into slits, widened his stance, and stared at me. I'd laughed. "Going to take me down?"

"Before retirement, I treated your daughter's Pomeranian. Wish I'd told her to take that yapping pain in the butt someplace else." He'd angled his body toward the door. *Good. The old fool's leaving.* But he hadn't. He'd turned, taken a run at me, and jabbed his shoulder into my chest. "Take that you smart aleck," Henry had said.

I'd pushed him away. "If you show up here again, I'll have you arrested. Get out!"

Henry's legs had moved faster than I'd imagined they could, but in his attempt to get out the door, his shoulder had brushed the doorframe. "Ouch! Might sue you for physical damage, also."

He barely made contact. Old fool's a fake, too. I had headed back to join Alex and our class. *Hope he's gone for good.*

I'd had my hand on the silver handle ready to enter the ballroom. But I'd stopped. An understanding my anger hadn't allowed me to consider minutes earlier had struck me. Henry's words, "your daughter's Pomeranian," had echoed. *Tom and Andrea took Spanky to him? Did he kill their dog? Nah. He's old. But . . . if he sedated Spanky he could. And then it would've been easy for him to do the kind of damage I witnessed.*

Chapter 29 - A Slug, a Stagger, a Fall and a Question Mark
Monday, July 17

I hadn't told Alex about my scheduled appointment with Commissioner Giovanni Fulcono, nor had I mentioned my suspicion that Dr. Henry Walsh might have killed Spanky. I had wanted to enjoy teaching with my wife, but guilt had dumped a load of tension on me. I had faked a sunny disposition, the best I could, during our morning classes.

At noon, I'd gotten my sandwich out of the refrigerator in our studio's small kitchen, and I had sat down at the table. *How should I tell Alex about my appointment?*

My notion about who killed Spanky had had to wait. *I'll call Tom later and ask if he or Andrea ever took Spanky to a veterinarian by the name of Walsh. Henry might have heard me mention their dog's name in class. Sly, old fart.*

"Why aren't you eating?" my wife had said.

"I'll eat later." *Might as well get right to it.* "Honey, I have an appointment at one o'clock, but I'll get back before our second afternoon class begins."

Alex's eyes had held steady on me. "An appointment? Where are you going?"

"To Commissioner Fulcono's office. I'm going to convince him to stop harassing Andrea."

"I don't know how you got an appointment, but if you think you can waltz into his office under false pretenses, you'll get thrown out. Or arrested. And if you accuse him of killing Spanky, he may sue us."

He'll have to get in line, had run through my mind. "I'll take my chances." Without having said anything else, I'd put my sandwich back in the refrigerator and left.

I'd gotten off the bus at Broadway and made my way to the Metropolitan Transportation Authority. In my head, I'd practiced what I'd say to Commissioner Fulcono. Words I wouldn't have wanted my wife to hear.

I'd entered the headquarters and located the floor-list plaque next to the elevator.

"May I help you?" a middle-aged woman seated at a desk had greeted me.

"I'm Tim Wells. I have an appointment with Commissioner Fulcono."

"Please have a seat," she'd motioned to a chair. "You're early, but I'll let him know you're here."

The secretary had called Commissioner Fulcono. "Commissioner, your one-o'clock appointment arrived." She had paused. "Okay." She'd hung up. "Second door on the right."

I hadn't had to knock. He'd had the door open. "Come in." He'd motioned for me to sit.

What, no handshake, no smile? Huh. Let's cut to the chase attitude.

"Mr. Wells, I've spent a considerable amount of time looking into your complaint about Thirty-fourth Street. Herald Square is a busy shopping area, I agree. But I've compared pedestrian accident and fatality numbers from January 2005 through June of 2005, with the same six months this year. They've dropped. A road reconfiguration isn't warranted." He'd tapped his pen on the desk.

A considerable amount of time? To look up statistics on his computer? His matter-of-fact attitude had struck me as cold. My self-control had crashed. "Well." I'd stood up and had banged my fist on his desk. "I'm taking too much of your precious time. I'd better cut to the chase. Thirty-fourth Street isn't the reason I'm here."

"Then what do you want?"

"My name isn't Wells, it's Partridge, and I demand you stop terrorizing my daughter, Andrea Warden."

The commissioner's face had exploded with awareness. "She's the lawyer trying to convict my son! Get out! Or I'll call the police!"

I had leaned over, and head-to-head with him I'd grabbed his shirt collar. "Leave her alone, or I'll put you in the hospital."

He'd grabbed the phone on his desk, lifted it from its cradle.

"Go ahead, call the police. I'll tell them how you mutilated Andrea's dog."

Giovanni Fulcono's olive-skinned, potholed face had twisted into shock. He'd stared back at me, and he had put the phone back on its cradle. He'd stood up. "I don't know what you're talking about. I haven't harmed anyone's dog." His line of sight had dropped down to the carpet, and a glassy sheen had covered his eyes. "My son's battling alcoholism. He's sick. His mother and I are beside ourselves about the cyclist's death. Michael needs medical help, not prison. And I'll do anything in my power to keep him from getting incarcerated."

Anything. There it is. "And I'll do anything to keep my daughter safe." I'd drawn back my fist and slugged him in the jaw. He'd staggered backward, and his chair had rolled with him. He had landed flat on his back, sprawled out on the floor. "That's a small taste of what I'm capable of doing to protect my daughter, Commissioner."

I had caught the bus back to The Silver Slipper. *Bet the police arrive before I do. He's crazy and has killed an innocent pet, but I bet I'm the one going to jail.*

I'd watched from the doorway. My devoted wife had had everything under control, and she'd been closing out intermediate waltz. "Practice at home. If you have no partner, ladies and gentlemen, review the steps you must perform by yourself. Have a good weekend, and I'll see you next Monday."

As I had entered, she'd smiled that special way that always made my heart speed up. *I'd better tell her before the police arrive.*

She'd taken me by the arm, and her kiss had distracted me. "I'm glad you're back. Teaching without you isn't the same. How'd it go with Commissioner Fulcono?"

"I punched him in the jaw, and he fell backward. I'm surprised the police aren't here now."

Her eyes had widened, and I'd waited for a reprimand. Instead, her eyes had twinkled, and her huge smile had thrown me off guard. She'd cradled my face with her hands. "Thank-you. I'm sorry. I was wrong. I'm glad you approached Commission Fulcono. He deserved a punch. Maybe he'll leave Andrea alone now. When the police come, we'll deal with this together." Alex's lips had enveloped mine. And I'd thought, *I'll love you through eternity.*

We'd finished our classes for the day, and the police hadn't shown up to arrest me. Though I had appreciated they hadn't, a puzzling question had dangled with me throughout the night. *Why didn't the Commissioner call them?* I'd decided only one answer had made sense. *He'd killed Spanky as a warning for Andrea to back off, and he doesn't want me to accuse him in front of the police.*

Chapter 30 - Rehearsal and Another Threat
Tuesday, July 18

Robert had arrived with his dancers for another 5:30 p.m. practice. *In eight days, we perform at Adelphi Performing Arts Center. I don't think we'll be ready. How can we have all the kinks ironed out?*

"Get dressed," my son had said. "Ladies use the bathroom. Guys the boutique, down the hall on the right." Alex and I had gone to our office to put on our costumes.

Our son had gathered the dance troupe together. "Listen up. Before tonight, you've danced in tights and T-shirts. This is the first practice in costume. Try to keep your hands and arms clear of the petals to avoid timing and balance problems. Michaela and Tyler take a seat on the park bench. Cherry blossoms, listen to the introductory music and sway in sync, as if a gentle breeze is blowing. On my cue, start the first dance movement."

The night before, I had tossed and turned. Not wanting to wake Alex, I'd finally gotten up. My visit to the commissioner had revisited me. And questions had jabbed at my role as Andrea's father. *Did I get my message across? Did Commissioner Fulcono understand I'd go as far as I needed to in order to protect her?*

By the end of practice, sleep deprivation had left me with a truth. My performance had stunk.

Praises had oozed like honey, sticky and sweet, from Robert's lips for everyone in the troupe, except me. But I'd had other things on my mind. Michael Fulcono's trial and Andrea's determination to get justice for David Bowman's family had collided with my concentration. And like I had stumbled through a blanket of fog from lack of sleep and anxiety, my missteps and clumsy movements had embarrassed me throughout the two hours of rehearsal.

I'd eaten up Alex's praise for my macho move, but his secretary had heard the ruckus, witnessed the commissioner sprawled out on the floor. *How stupid of me. I didn't think before I acted. He could still have me arrested. Why hasn't he? He plans to kill Andrea. And he doesn't want suspicion thrown his way.*

She can't convict Michael Fulcono. Alex and I can't change her mind. Tom can't, either. God, please persuade her to lose the case. Or at least cause her to botch her prosecution. Yeah, right. Like that's going to happen.

Alex had gone to the office to take off her costume. Robert had approached me. "What's the matter with you tonight?"

"Trouble sleeping."

"Dad, a lot is going on, I get that. Mom's told me about the threats to Andrea. I'm worried about my sister. I called her and tried to persuade her to drop the case, but she told me to mind my own business. If you perform like you did tonight at Adelphi, Dad, we won't get applause, we'll get booed. Get your act together. Please."

Robert's tensed, red face had sent me a message. *He's angry. His heart's in saving The Silver Slipper. And he's right. If I don't get my head screwed on straight, I'll blow our opportunity. I shouldn't have kept Robert's or Angela's families out of the loop about the threats to Andrea's life.*

My options to protect Andrea had dwindled. I'd thought of approaching other members of the NYC Transit Port Authority for help. But reality had hit me, like a ton of bricks. *Why would they believe me?*

The likelihood of losing The Silver Slipper had jarred plans Alex and I had had for the future. But Andrea's life in jeopardy had turned our world upside down. *If she dies, part of me and her mother dies, too.*

Alex and I had caught the train. Homeward bound, my wife had rested her head on my shoulder. She'd heard Robert's reprimand to me, and I'd guessed she had thought it best to let me lick my wounds in quiet.

My phone had rung, jarring me from my thoughts. "Hi, Tom. What's up?" Alex had moved her ear close to my phone.

"Andrea told me at dinner she'd received more threatening phone calls. She said the caller's gruff voice had again sounded phony. And she couldn't identify whether it was a man or a woman."

I could tell her which one. "Given the trial she's involved in, don't you think she should have an idea who it is?" My ears and neck had heated.

"Yes," Tom replied. "But she can't prove it, Ty."

"Did she report the phone calls to the police?"

"No. I asked her to, but she wouldn't. Instead, she talked to a coworker at the DA's Vehicular Crime Office. He told her to ask the police department to assign a plainclothes cop to tail her."

"Did she do that?"

"No. And she won't hand the bridge case off to another attorney, either. Ty, you know as well as I do that Andrea loves a challenging fight."

"Yeah. She's a scrapper."

"What if something happens to her?" Tom's voice had cracked with emotion. "Don't tell her I called."

"I won't but keep me posted." I'd hung up. Both fear for my daughter's life and anger for the commissioner's threat had risen up in me.

Tears had run down Alex's cheeks. Her pleading eyes had focused on me. "Isn't there anything we can we do?"

"I'll pay the commissioner another visit, Honey."

"Please don't go back to his office, Ty. He'll have you arrested."

"Okay, I won't." *I'll pay him a call somewhere else*, had entered my mind. And in the moment, the somewhere else had flashed like a neon sign in my head.

Chapter 31 - What Else?
Thursday, July 20

I hadn't spoken to my parents for a while, and I'd decided to check in with them before Alex and I had started our first class. Mom had answered. Her flat, soft, "hello," had gotten my attention.

What's she down in the dumps about? "Hi Mom. Everything okay?"

A heavy sigh had set me ill at ease. "No. It's your dad," her voice had quivered. "Charles's glucose level is too high."

A flashback of my dad lying in Wakefield Memorial Hospital Intensive Care in '78' had revisited me. He'd had two strokes and required speech and physical therapy as part of his rehab. But worse than his physical problems, he'd had a battle with depression. "He's in the hospital?"

"No, at home. His doctor put him on a different anticoagulant. Put restrictions on his diet, too. And he's scheduled to get frequent blood tests. He didn't want me to . . . say anything to you or Alex."

"Okay. I'll play dumb if Dad answers the phone when I call. But if his condition worsens, you'll let me know?"

"I will."

"Mom, if he needs a hospital, take him to Barnes-Jewish. It's larger, better equipped."

"Okay. It's good to hear from you. We love you, Ty."

"I love you guys, too." I'd hung up. *She has her hands full. If I lived closer, I could help.*

I had entered Ballroom One weighted with another worry. In the midst of teaching, a stranger had entered the ballroom. I had walked toward him and left Alex to handle the class.

"Are you Ty Partridge?"

"Yes. What can I do for you?"

He'd handed me an envelope. "You've been summoned to appear in court." Without saying anything else, he'd left.

I'd torn open the envelope. My eyes had scanned the summons, gotten to the meat of the document: United States District Court for Plaintiff, Dr. Henry Walsh v. Defendant, Ty Partridge.

That old fool. I'd read on, gotten to the particulars of the summons. Within twenty-one days, not counting that Thursday, I had to provide an answer to the plaintiff or his lawyer and file an answer or motion with the court.

Well, Henry Walsh, Doctor of Veterinary Medicine, here's your answer. Go ahead and sue. I'll show up in court with my lady witnesses from dance class. They'll tell how you sexually harassed Maria.

I'd read on. *Thank goodness the court date won't interfere with our performance. But if somehow the old fool wins, Alex and I lose our livelihood.* As if I'd crossed paths with a black cat multiple times, my plate had overflowed with problems. *What else can possibly happen?*

I had taken my place next to Alex. "What did that man want?" she'd asked.

"He served us a summons. Henry Walsh is suing us."

Chapter 32 - A Full Plate
Thursday, July 27

We'd left our apartment and had caught the train. Alex's phone had rung. "Hello," she answered. Then, "Calm down. I can't understand you." An intense, glazed hardness had filled her eyes, and a tunnel had burrowed between her eyebrows. "What? But you're doing your work at home."

I hadn't had to ask who had called.

"You'll find a better job. She doesn't deserve a dedicated employee like you. Besides, Andrew makes a good living. You don't need to rush to find one."

Alex's ear had remained pressed against her phone, and her stern eyes had communicated hostility. "I understand. But get ahold of yourself. Do you want me to help with Abigail? Your dad can teach solo."

My wife had paused.

"One of the ladies, who follows well."

Alex, I don't want to teach with a student, had popped into my head.

"Okay. Yes, I hear Abigail crying. I'll call you tonight. Love you." Alex had hung up.

"What a witch! Mrs. Schrader fired our daughter. She has no concern for anyone but herself. Not for Angela, not for our colicky, little granddaughter."

I had put my arm around my wife. "I'm glad Angela isn't working for the old, redheaded coot anymore. She'd left me with a bad impression at the baby shower." *I wish I had asked her where she parked her broom.*

"Angela's body needs to recover from the pregnancy," Alex had said. "Thank goodness Mrs. Schrader didn't have any children. I can't imagine how they'd have turned out."

"I agree with you on both counts. Our daughter deserves a nicer work environment, a nicer employer. Don't worry. She'll find one, Honey."

We'd finished our day at The Silver Slipper. I'd gotten busy writing checks for bills approaching their due date. Robert had poked his head in the office. "Dancers are arriving, Dad."

He'd left, and the phone in the office had rung. "Hello." I had heard breathing, but no response. "Who is this?"

"Is this Ty Partridge?"

Obvious, fake accent. The person who called me before? Don't think so. "Yes?"

"I'm an informant with an important message. The person threatening your daughter has spent time in a mental institution. Tell the lawyer to throw the case. Otherwise, she'll die."

Alex had come looking for me, and I'd hung up. "Ty, everyone's waiting."

Confused, I'd followed my wife into the ballroom. *Two days till performance. Concentrate. Get it right*, I'd repeated in my head, like a chant. But when I had stepped onto my foothold, a different mantra had overridden. *Andrea can't die, she can't, she can't.*

Chapter 33 - Return of the Spirits
Still Thursday, July 27

I had tossed and turned. Scenarios of how to protect Andrea had looped over and over in my head. *I have no choice but to disable the man. Then he can't harm her.* Alex had rolled from her back onto her side. *I don't want to wake her.* I had rotated my body and gotten to a seated position on the edge of the bed. I'd started to stand, and a hand had taken hold of my arm and helped me up. Startled, I'd faced Reverend Maynard, who'd stood almost nose to nose with me. The reverend's hand had grasped my arm, or I'd have fallen backward. My sister Allison's spirit had materialized next to the preacher, and they'd escorted me to the living room.

Overwhelmed, I'd hugged my sister. "I've missed you."

"I've missed you, too." She'd placed her hand on my cheek. "Cancel the performance, Bird. Please."

"Why would you say that? It's my one and only chance to save the dance studio."

Allison had locked eyes with Reverend Maynard, as if she'd needed his approval to speak. And the silence could have been cut with a knife. The reverend had nodded, given her the okay. "You're human," her voice had quivered with emotion. "You can't foresee what–"

"Enough!" the reverend had shouted. "You've said all you can. We must go." With those words, both spirits had disappeared.

I'd sat on the couch. *Why did my sister act the way she did? Why had her voice trembled? Does she think the performance will flop? Is she trying to protect Alex and me from humiliation? This is our one shot to save our studio.* Her lack of confidence in me, Alex, and Robert, had cut me to the bone. *Well, little sister, you still think of me as that lanky kid you called Bird. So, I hope you're watching Saturday night. Our dance troupe is going to bring the house to their feet.*

Chapter 34 - The Performance
Saturday Evening, July 29

The Japanese cherry blossom trees had stood naked, stripped of their pink flowers on Adelphi University's Garden City Campus. Their season had passed. I'd recalled how months earlier Robert had told his mother about the beautiful blossoms. "A sight to see," he had said. And I had wished I'd seen them at the peak of their season.

At 5:30, the wet sidewalk had dampened our shoes, and a flash of white had streaked through the gray sky. A clap of thunder, its partner, had followed. *Please, God. No more rain, or not many will come.*

Alex and I had entered the Performing Arts Center. Stressed about the performance, I had clammed up, but my wife had rattled on and on, and I'd guessed that was her way of coping with her nerves.

A woman in a gaudy, geometric-pattern blouse and tight, stretch jeans had walked past us, and Alex had stopped talking. Her spiky, black hair had added to what I'd guessed was her attempt to look younger. And a man with shoulder-length, gray hair, who had worn black rimmed glasses, had accompanied her. "Let me carry the briefcase for you," he'd said, and had attempted to take the handle. The woman's large, triangular earrings had swung frantically, as the man had attempted to take the case from her. But she'd held onto it. "No thank you. I'm quite capable of carrying it myself."

Alex had turned to me, "Cranky old gal. And that hair. Dressed ridiculous, too."

I had laughed. "Faculty from the Art Department?"

"That's my guess. Might have had an exhibition on campus earlier," Alex had said.

We'd entered the dance theatre. I had imagined the staggered rows of red seats filled to capacity, but in the next second reality had reeled me in. *Half of the seats occupied would be great.*

Robert had stood next to Brandon on the stage. As Alex and I had approached, our son's taut features had relaxed. He'd smiled and waved at us.

"Everything okay?" I had said.

"Yes, of course. Brandon has his student helpers tweaking the lighting for color variation and dramatic effect. I wanted them to adjust something. The projector's already been tested, and it's working great. We have to have those aphids show up on the screen, don't we," Robert had said. "Sorry Dad, gotta go; I need to talk to Brandon about one more thing I want tweaked."

The moment had turned real for me, but it had also turned back time, a time when performing on stage had dangled like a carrot in front of me. Young and ambitious, I had grabbed the opportunity, and my absence as a father of young children had taken its toll on my wife. My foolishness had almost cost me my marriage. I'd wrapped my arm around Alex's waist and pulled her to me. "I love you. Break a leg tonight, Alex."

"I love you more. Even though you're so superstitious."

"Aren't you going to wish me good luck?"

"Nope. You don't need it."

Inside my head a clock had ticked, closing in on performance time, and I'd had one regret. I had wanted our whole family to attend. Angela had had to stay home with Abbey. Otherwise, Andrew would have had his hands full dealing with a colicky baby alone. Tom had had babysitting duty, too. *My girls got themselves good men*, I'd reflected. *At least Andrea can come.*

Robert had returned to the stage, and other troupe members had hurried past us carrying their costumes. "Mom and Dad, follow them to the dressing areas. Two students are backstage to do your makeup. When you're done, have the dance troupe, Tyler, and Michaela come out to the stage with you.

"We dismantled the tree to move it here. I want to test it for stability before the seats start to fill for the performance."

The curtain had remained closed. We'd taken the stage and mounted our footholds on the tree. The buds, Kami and Brian, costumed in light green body suits and tights, had each worn one delicate, pale pink sprout attached to their pale green hood. Their costumes had emitted an air of innocence as they'd mounted their footholds in the center, the safest place on the tree.

Alex and I, adult cherry blossoms, had been outfitted in white petals, two of which had contained brown spots. And our sage green tights and body suits had had a hint of gray, which had also symbolized our downward descent toward aging. Our footholds, close to the buds, had placed us in a strategic position to protect them.

The young flowers, Amy and Lisa, had worn bright pink flowers, with pea green tights and bodysuits. They had mounted the next footholds around the tree.

Stephanie and Dave, the teens, had taken the outer branches. Vibrant, medium-sized, pink petals, and their emerald green tights had emphasized their vitality and their ability to serve as protectors of the elderly, Lauren and Matt. The gray petals worn by the aged cherry blossoms, and their lackluster tights, the color of seaweed, had designated them as the most deteriorated and vulnerable members of the family.

"Everyone hold your positions," Robert had said.

My legs had begun to quiver. *That's long enough*, I'd thought. But certain mere minutes had passed, I'd figured my keyed-up state had deceived me. *Calm down. I can't mess this up.*

With my son's words, "Good. The tree is solid. Dismount," the tremors in my leg muscles had stopped. "Rest until we mount for the performance," he'd said. "And keep your hands off of the makeup."

Michaela, dressed in a floral-patterned kimono, with a pink sash, had sat next to Tyler on their stage prop, a park bench. Tyler dressed in blue shorts, a striped red and blue T-shirt and tennis shoes, had looked like the typical kid, dressed for play. Angled toward the Japanese cherry blossom tree, the audience had had a clear view of the Japanese Grandmother, her grandson, and the tree.

In my ecstatic state, I had had no desire to sit. I'd parted the stage's curtain and watched Adelphi students hand out programs. And I had imagined the audience's response to our performance. My mind's eye had created their soul-searching faces, painted with remorse, for time past and not well spent. Time they'd never get back. I'd imagined their tearful eyes, their faraway gazes, as they'd reached back in time and remembered deceased loved ones who had brought joy into their lives. But I had envisioned something more, something which had to leave an imprint on everyone in the theatre. Dance of Cherry Blossoms had to ring true the unavoidable reality of their own mortality.

My mind's eye had taken a sudden halt. In had walked Dr. Henry Walsh. *The old dance Casanova. What's he doing here? He'll make a scene and ruin everything*. I had approached Robert and pointed out Henry from our vantage spot, the stage's parted curtain. "Don't worry, Dad. I'll tell one of the ushers to keep an eye on him. If he gets out of line, he'll get escorted out."

At 7:55 the lights had flickered. We'd all mounted our footholds behind the closed curtain. My heart had beat like a drum, and my stomach had churned. Yes, I'd had a bad case of the jitters. About the audiences' reaction. About Henry wrecking our big night.

I'd looked at Alex, who'd looked composed. "I love you," she'd mouthed from her foothold on the tree.

"I love you more," I'd mouthed back.

"Thank-you for attending our performance this evening. My name is Robert Partridge. I'm a dance instructor at Adelphi University of Performing Arts, and I'm happy to announce our dance chair, Mrs. Myra Rand, is in the audience. Without her, this performance wouldn't have happened. Myra, would you please stand? Let's give her a round of applause."

The clapping had stopped. Robert continued, "The dance troupe this evening consists of Adelphi students enrolled in my classes, and students enrolled at The Silver Slipper Dance Studio, instructed by my talented parents, Ty and Alexandra Partridge. On the back of your program, there's a bio about my parents' lengthy dance history and details about lessons given at their studio. Without further ado, I present to you *Dance of Cherry Blossoms*."

The curtains had parted, and we'd held our poses on our footholds. The lighting had focused on two Adelphi University students who'd carried a sign downstage center: Scene One - The Beginning of a Thorny Lesson.

The students had exited, and the house lights had dimmed. Instrumental music had begun, and bright lighting had simulated sunshine. An elderly Japanese woman and a young boy had sat on a park bench. A wide sleeve of the woman's floral kimono had draped across the young boy's shoulder as she'd hugged him. Her large, straw purse had sat on the bench next to her.

The instrumental music had softened, faded away. "Grandson, do you remember the Japanese word I taught you for grandmother?"

"Of course. Sobo."

"That's right. You listened well." She'd smiled and patted his arm. "And what is the word for grandson?"

"Magomusuko," he'd said and grinned.

"You are an excellent student. Today, I will teach you a thorny lesson. I want you to use your imagination while I tell you a story about Japanese cherry blossoms." She'd pointed at a tree situated near their bench. "Sakura, the delicate pink flowers of that tree brighten the world with their beauty during their short life."

"A story about a *tree and flowers*, Sobo?"

"Yes."

Magomusuko had shrugged his shoulders. "Sounds boring."

A tender smile had shown on her face. "Play along, please. Open your ears and heart. Listen to the gentle breeze."

An audio of soft swishing sounds had begun. "See how the breeze blows and rustles the tree's flowers, creating a calming melody."

The young boy had leaned forward, listened. "Yes, I hear it."

As though they were one, two buds had cuddled and demonstrated affection.

"Can you see the new sprouts snuggling?" Sobo had said.

The boy had remained silent, mulled over her question. He'd smiled and answered with an affirmative nod. "Like babies do?"

"Yes. You used to nestle your head on my shoulder, then you drifted off to sleep."

"I think the buds are going to sleep," her magomusuko had said.

"Perhaps," she had replied. "Those buds will open and turn into small flowers, like human babies develop into a small child."

"Ah, look! The buds played possum," his grandmother had continued. They had erected themselves and bent down and up in quick movements. "Their feigned sleep was nothing more than a game."

Instrumental music had pulsated with life. The young and teen cherry blossoms had sprung into action, shaken their petals rapidly in beat with the music, and their stems had stretched up toward the bright, orange sun, shown on the backdrop screen. The buds had erected themselves and attempted to replicate their movements. But smaller and lacking strength, their attempts had fallen short, and they bumped into one another.

The grandson had winked at his sobo. "They're clumsy, Sobo. I hope they don't fall."

The adults had swayed back and forth, and they'd kept beat with the music. The elderly had joined in, but they'd swayed at a slower tempo. And soon the stems of the senior flowers had assumed a stooped posture, and they'd ceased to move.

The instrumental music had grown sluggish. And the buds had rocked back-and-forth. They had staggered, like drunken sailors, and finally, their stems had bowed toward the ground.

"Yes. The young buds don't have a lot of endurance or strength," the grandmother continued. "See how the teens and adults pirouette to form barriers around them. They're keep enemies away from the exhausted sprouts."

The young and teen flowers, still full of vigor, had leaped up and spun in circles, as if dancing to a much faster beat. "Watching them spin makes me dizzy, Sobo," the grandson giggled. "You'd tell me to slow down if I danced like that."

"You don't remember, but I protected you when you were much younger. Like the buds, you had to grow steady on your feet and learn to keep your balance. And I hope I've taught you that enemies exist who would try to harm you."

The adults had slowed their movements. And the elder cherry blossoms had danced as if they couldn't hear the music's beat. But the boy's eyes had remained fixed on his grandmother. "You still take good care of me," he'd said in earnest.

The sobo had wiped at her eyes.

"What's wrong?" the grandson had asked.

"Nothing. Your love touches my heart. You are a wonderful grandson."

The instrumental music had gotten faster, turned playful, and coaxed the buds to make another attempt to dance. With awkward movements, they'd fallen over onto their sides. They had struggled to straighten their small petals, and they'd managed to erect themselves. But unsure of their connection to the tree, the buds had collided into each other.

"Did they bump noggins?" asked the grandson.

"Yes," the grandmother had smiled while bumping heads with her magomusuko. And they'd both laughed. The music's tempo had grown slower, and the volume softened, like that of a lullaby. The buds had leaned into each other.

"Sobo?" Magomusuko's forehead had wrinkled. "Are they hurt?"

"No. But like human babies, they need a nap."

The two adult cherry blossoms had moved closer to the buds. Magomusuko had turned toward his grandmother. "What are the adults doing?"

"Watch. They'll use their stems to hunker down." One adult had squatted behind the young buds, and the other adult had crouched in front of them. They'd turned their feet outward to form a plié. And the buds' petals had collapsed down toward their stems.

"The buds are hurt Sobo!"

No, they are resting." She'd hugged her grandson. "Don't worry. The adults won't leave the blossoms. It's their job to keep them safe."

The young grandson had smiled. "Like you've kept me safe, Sobo."

She had wiped runaway tears from her cheeks.

Her grandson had taken hold of her free hand, and he'd pointed with his other. "Look! Enemies attack."

"The adult blossoms straighten their stems," she'd said. "Do you see them spin around and around, in a pirouette?"

"I do," he'd said. "They strike at the enemy with their stems."

"Good. They've chased those aphids away."

Magomusuko had nodded in affirmation and continued to play along.

The other pink flowers had shaken their petals. The dancers had moved their arms in waves across their torsos to block another attempted assault on members of their family.

The adult cherry blossoms had faced one another. They'd stood on their right leg and stretched their left leg out straight behind them to form an arabesque. The dancers' clasped hands had formed a protective canopy over the buds.

"They stand guard over their babies, protecting them from those insects," the sobo had said. "They must watch for caterpillars and Japanese beetles that might attack, too."

Frightened and not fully developed, the young flowers had shaken. But the teens, full of vitality, had leaped into action and thrown kicks to help rescue the buds.

"You, Mom, and Dad, protect me," the grandson had said.

"Yes," the sobo had responded. "Your parents are worthy protectors, and I try my best. Look. Do you see the rest of the family rejoicing? The young, the teens, and the elderly? Each age dances in their own way. The buds are safe, and they are celebrating."

Magomusuko had looked the tree over. "Yes. I see them. All the flowers show their happiness." He'd pointed at the tree. "I bet those are teenagers. They shake and bend their stems up and down. Their movements are weird."

"Look at those two young ones," the sobo had pointed, and she'd encouraged his vivid imagination.

"They act like Jack-in-the boxes, Sobo. I used to have one with a clown that popped up. But I had to push him back down, or he wouldn't pop up again. Those two do it over and over, without help. I see all the members of the family. And like humans, each age group acts differently."

She'd hugged him. "So young, but wise."

"That's the end of the story, Sobo?"

"Not quite. The new buds and other beautiful pink flowers call that tree home. But one day each of the flowers will grow old, like me. When that happens, they contribute to the family in another way, with wisdom. Close your eyes. Imagine them with brown spots and wrinkles. Like me."

He'd shut his eyes. "I can't see them. Help me, Sobo."

She had taken hold of his left hand with her right. They'd stood and faced one another. "Follow my lead. You will understand old age." The music had lumbered along, as if burdened with enormous weight. The sobo's choppy, sluggish steps had forced her magomusuko to follow suit. And as if over and over he'd stepped in a rut and attempted recovery, his awkward steps had mimicked hers well.

The other flowers had joined in the lethargic, irregular movements his sobo had demonstrated.

"It's like wearing concrete shoes, and I can't control my balance," he'd said.

A breeze had blown, and his grandmother had staggered. Her grandson had imitated her lead and rocked back on his heels. In the next moment, the wind's momentum had changed, gained energy. His sobo had hunkered down to avoid losing her balance. He'd crouched down beside her and emulated her struggle against the wind's force. Exhausted, she'd puffed. "When one gets old, wisdom must balance a lack of strength. Time to rest."

A petal splattered with brown had fallen from each of the adult cherry blossoms and drifted down to the ground. "Losing those petals has made them clumsy, Magomusuko. They cannot keep their stems straight. And soon they'll lose more petals."

"They are weaker, Sobo?"

"Yes. The aging process is at work. They wobble, like me. Now, they are elderly flowers."

Nearby beetles had landed in the tree. "Watch. They'll try to take advantage of the family's weakened security," his sobo had said.

The unprotected buds had shivered with fear. The elderly had thrown weak kicks and attempted to ward off the attack on the frantic, inexperienced sprouts. The teens had joined in to help. They'd executed harder kicks while pivoting counterclockwise to combat the swarm of beetles.

The instrumental music had slowed, turned melancholy. "The elderly flowers' energy is spent," the sobo had said. "The old flowers shed more and more decayed petals, and they lose more and more strength, until one day those cherry blossoms no longer exist."

"No more sadness. Please, Sobo."

She'd forced a smile, and the music had changed to an energetic beat.

"Watch. I'll dance like a teenager," he'd said. But his unrefined coordination had lacked precision. His face had turned red. He hadn't succeeded, hadn't mimicked the teens' movements. "I can't do it. No more pretending."

"You have the right to get bored with my dance. But do not get upset about the dance of teenagers. I cannot keep up with them, either. Their dance is in your future, but for me it is in the past."

The wind had calmed. The instrumental music had softened, slowed.

"Ah, the elderly Japanese cherry blossoms attempt to dance again," the sobo had said. "I have rested. This I can manage." Her wide sleeves had inched up, exposing her thin arms. Though no resistance had existed, her arms had swayed in uneven waves, like bumps in the air impeded them. But she'd smiled.

"Watch, young magomusuko." The teen blossoms had jumped up and landed on their branches over and over again. "They refuse the sluggish music. See them shaking their petals, uninhibited? They protest by dancing to a different beat."

"How silly they look complaining," he'd said and winked. The tempo had remained slow, and he'd imitated his grandmother's wavy arm movements, but he hadn't tried to outdo her. A wide smile had shown on his face, and his eyes had lit up like two fireflies. "I love you, Sobo."

"And I love you. Your turn to shine. Frolic to music you create in your head. I do not need to instruct you. I must rest." With an uneven, slow gait, she had returned to the park bench. The magomusuko's shoulders had shimmied. His imagination had visualized the young cherry blossoms dancing, and it had spurred him on to uninhibited movement.

His sobo had called out, "Come rest awhile." He'd sat with her on the park bench, laid his head against her shoulder, and they'd both fallen asleep.

The stage had darkened, ending Scene One, and the curtain had closed. Applause from the audience had rung throughout the theatre.

After the clapping had died down, the curtain had reopened. The lighting had focused downstage center, highlighting the two Adelphi students, who'd held another sign: Scene Two: The Storm.

The lighting had dimmed, and the two students had exited. The stage had brightened, and playful instrumental music had played.

"Do you see the buds shaking their petals in play, Magomusuko?" the grandmother had said, seated next to her grandson on the bench.

"Yes," he'd replied. "And look. They've bent over and collapsed into a tight fold. And now, they stand upright again. But they stagger from side to side."

"The buds are attempting to keep time with the music," she'd said.

The stage lighting had darkened, and the lighthearted music had turned solemn, like funeral music. And this time many enemies had attacked the buds. Aphids, caterpillars, and Japanese beetles had swarmed around the small sprouts. The buds had squatted and gone into a doubled over posture. They'd rocked from side to side.

The adult flowers had attacked. They'd stood on one leg, the other bent behind into a backward L-shape, and they'd kicked at the intruders, who had attempted to harm the youngest members of the family, the buds. The aged had kicked at the enemies, too, but their contacts had had little clout. Teenagers had joined in the fight. Their vigorous wallops had scared the caterpillars and Japanese beetles away. But the young, panic-stricken buds had remained doubled over, and they had shaken with fear.

Magomusuko had played along. He'd tensed his forehead. "Two enemies remain," he'd shouted. "Look how big they are, Sobo. They'll kill the little buds."

She'd tried to stifle a smile. "Do not fear for the buds. The adults and teens stand their ground. They continue to kick the aphids."

"Aphids?"

"Bad insects. They give flowers a virus," she had said. "And like with humans, the virus can pass to the rest of the family. If that happens, all the flowers die. That's why the cherry blossom flowers must chase the aphids away."

Depleted of energy from the battle to protect the buds, a petal splashed with brown had dropped from both of the adult cherry blossoms. "They age more," his sobo had said.

"See how the elderly sway back and forth on their outer branches," she continued. "They are upset. They lament their weakened state. They understand their strength comes in spurts, and then they must rest. They must not lose the petals they have left. When those fall, they'll perish."

"Perish?" her magomusuko had said.

"They'll die."

The grandson's eyes had sobered. "But I don't want them to."

The instrumental music had changed, quickened, and the sobo had asked in reply, "Do you see how fast the teens dance?"

The young boy's face had brightened with hope. "Yes. Can they scare the aphids away?"

"Maybe. But if they don't, and the enemy strikes the fragile buds harder, they'll kill them," his sobo had said.

The aging flowers had gotten a burst of energy and struck again at the aphids. Furious about their invasion, they'd kicked at the intruders. But with petals gone, their awkward movements had thrown them off-balance. And spent from exhaustion, the elderly had had no fight left in them. But the aphids hadn't given up.

The teens, full of energy, had come to the rescue, and the aphids had left. The cherry blossom tree had remained safe, again. But the sense of security hadn't lasted long. The sky had darkened, and thunderous claps had shaken the cherry blossoms. The flowers had cowered in fear. A new attack, one with gusty wind, pelting rain, thunder, and flashes of lightning, had threatened to cast the hunkered down, swaying flowers from the tree. "A bad storm has arrived, my young magomusuko. The cruel wind bullies us."

"Sobo, the rain distorts my sight." Her grandson had used his hands as canopies for his eyes.

The backdrop screen had shown that all the flowers had leaned into the turbulent storm's slanted rain. But the elderly hadn't had the power to protect themselves from the gale's wind. It had whipped the elderly and detached another petal from each of them. And they had fallen from their branches and landed lifeless on the ground.

The sobo had directed her magomusuko to help her turn the park bench over. "We must get under this for shelter. See the remaining flowers shake with fear?"

His sobo had narrowed her eyes to see through the slats of the bench. "Look at the buds fighting the wind's hostile roar. See how the adult blossoms have bent their stems forward to shelter them with their petals. They remain safe. Out of love, they risk their lives for the younger flowers. Out of love, I have sheltered you the best I can."

One bud protected by the adults had remained secure, but the other had swayed to-and-fro in jerky spasms, as it had fought to survive. And the wind's fierce force had beat down on the adults, and they had lost their grasps. Torn from its branch and in a state of panic, the bud had shuddered as it was swept away from its family. It had hit the ground and laid still as a stone at the foot of the tree. "The adult protectors, despite their determination, couldn't hold onto the one tender bud," the sobo had said.

The larger of the adult protectors had thrashed from side to side in agony for its ineptness to protect the bud. The other had drawn into itself, frozen in anguish. The teens had whipped their petals against the tree's branches to punish themselves for the deaths of their elders. Exhausted, they'd hung limp. And the remaining family members' stems had drooped with sorrow. "I wish the bud hadn't died, Sobo."

"I know you do, Magomusuko. You have a good heart."

The storm had ceased. A blue sky and the sun had returned on the backdrop screen. The young magomusuko had pushed with all his might to right the park bench. His sobo had hugged him. "You are a strong young man. But you are my grandson, and I worry about your safety. That's why I told you the cherry blossom story. When I'm swept away from the family tree, I must know I did everything in my power to teach you how to survive. The world has harsh winds and rain. You are my little bud. I want you to stay out of harm's way. Why do you think I tell you, 'Look before crossing the street. Choose friends who won't get you into trouble.'"

His eyes had held steady on her, and he had looked as if he'd soaked in everything she'd said. He had snuggled his sobo, and his body had trembled. "The bud's dead. That's not fair."

His sobo had nodded in agreement. She'd caressed his face with her hands. "Tragedy strikes humans, also. A child dies, and the family weeps. Outward weeping stops, but in the heart it never ends. We remember each flower that died, like I remember my danna. But I'll love my husband forever. The remaining family must move on and enjoy the rest of their lives. This I expect of you." She had pointed, "Look at the adults on the tree. They are okaasans, and otousans, mothers and fathers." Her magomusuko had directed his attention to the tree. "Look at the elderly flowers, lying dead on the ground. Before they died, they lost petals, like we old people lose hair. I've grown old."

He had grabbed her arm. "No! We're pretending. You must never leave me."

She'd released her hold on his face, kissed his forehead. "The sunshine brightens their world again, like you've brightened mine. And the remaining cherry blossom flowers move forward with living."

The adults had risen up on their toes, and in their exhausted, bowed state they'd managed poorly executed pirouettes. "The adults have lost strength, Magomusuko, but they have resumed their duty guarding the one tender bud left." The remaining flowers had performed an arabesque. They had stood on one leg and kept the other straight out behind. And they'd stretched their arms toward the remaining bud. They'd formed a barrier around it.

The sobo had sat down on the bench, and her magomusuko had approached the tree. He had run one hand across a place on its trunk, and he'd wiped at his eye with the other. "I'm sorry some members of your family died," he'd whispered.

He'd turned to go join his sobo. Her slumped head had hung toward her knees. He had run to her, placed his hands on her slouched back. "Sobo! Get up! Tell me the end of the story. Please."

She'd sat up, opened her eyes. "I'm sorry I frightened you, but I must rest." Her eyes had fluttered like a bird's flapping wings and then shut.

The dancers had held their poses and the lighting had gone up. Applause had sounded, and the curtain had closed.

Robert had used the stage's side entrance and stood downstage. "We'll have a fifteen-minute intermission. Bathroom facilities are located out in the hallway. Signs are posted to direct you."

The theatre lights had gone up and focused on the two Adelphi students holding another sign, Scene Three: Death and Renewal.

Seated on the park bench, the young boy had straightened his bent knees. He'd let them swing back-and-forth, back-and-forth. His grandmother's eyes had fluttered open.

"Ah, my short nap has refreshed me, Magomusuko. I guess you are anxious to hear the end of my story."

He'd stopped swinging his legs. "Yes. But I hope the rest is happy."

"We'll see. But to help you understand the remainder of the cherry blossoms' story, I will first tell you a shorter story about shoes."

The boy's face had conveyed confusion. "Shoes?"

"Yes. Be patient and listen. Shoes get old, used up. Weaken with holes. They can no longer serve their intended purpose."

"Sobo, I want to hear the end of the story about the cherry blossom tree."

"I promise you will."

Her young magomusuko had shifted on the bench and sighed.

She'd put her arm around the boy and continued her story. "If a pair of shoes wears out, you must get a new pair to replace the old ones, right?"

The young grandson had confirmed with a nod of agreement. "Mom bought me these new tennis shoes." He had lifted up his feet to show her.

"Very nice. Your okaasan takes good care of you. She wants your feet protected, shielded from cold, stones, and rain. Yes?"

A loud clap of thunder had prompted the cherry blossoms to jump up, and their hazardous landing had left them shaking with fear on their branches. The remaining blossoms had cowered, shrunken into tight balls. Magomusuko had shuddered at the thunder's unexpected return. "The thunder teases us, but I don't think the storm will return," his sobo had said. The boy had smiled, as if to confirm confidence in his grandmother's words. "I must finish my shoe story," she had said.

"But this has nothing–"

"Ah, but it does. Let me finish. Promise to not interrupt?"

The young boy had released a sigh of resignation. "Okay."

"Good. I took care of my musume when she was little. Now she takes care of you, your father, and me. I am the *old* shoe, scuffed by life's blows, threadbare, like those worn tennis shoes your mother replaced. I am the withered cherry blossom flower."

Her magomusuko's bottom lip had trembled, and a raspy groan had forced its way out. He'd shaken his head back-and-forth. "No. You're not. When my mother and father go to work, you take care of me."

The remaining members of the cherry blossom family had had bent stems, weighted by sorrow for the grandson's anguish.

"Once I considered myself a good sobo. But old age robs me of strength. You pour my tea, so I don't burn myself. You bring my slippers and put them on my feet. I can't bend to reach them. You allow me to tell you stories instead of playing with other children. I steal your childhood. And when we leave Central Park, you hold my hand walking home, pretending you need my guidance. But you do it to steady me in case I stumble. Now, you protect and care for me."

The grandson had denied her words, weighted with truth. "Not true."

The adult cherry blossoms had arched their stems into hyperextension and made inverted U's toward the one bud that remained on the tree, to guard it.

"I can no longer protect and take care of you, beloved Magomusuko."

"That's not true. I love you, Sobo. I don't mind pouring your tea or helping you with your slippers. And I like spending time with you." He'd rested his hand on top of hers.

"And I love you for it. Now, I will tell you how the cherry blossom story ends."

The boy's face had brightened, and he'd focused on his grandmother.

The adult blossoms had begun a happy dance. Their synchronized, rippling movements, like flowing waves, had passed from one cherry blossom to another, until all the remaining family had engaged. "The tree celebrates saving the one bud, and those flowers that remain cherish having another day of life," the sobo had said.

Rays of sunshine had bathed the cherry blossoms with warmth, and hypnotized by this comfort, their dancing had slowed. Their rise and fall movements had changed into a sluggish, wavy current, like the trickling flow of a stream. "Laziness sets in, Magomusuko." The cherry blossom flowers had stretched up on their toes, and their petals had fluttered, as if they'd yawned. They'd swayed from side to side, and they had collapsed into sleep.

"Do you think this should be the ending, Magomusuko?"

"I . . . guess. The remaining flowers look content. Does something else happen?"

"I'm afraid so. Watch." The instrumental music had turned gloomy, desperate. Lightening had charged through the sky. Charcoal gray clouds, in jagged shapes, had shown on the backdrop screen. The sound of wind had shrieked and spread throughout the theatre. And the adult cherry blossoms had squatted, like cowards.

"None of the flowers are protecting the one remaining bud," the grandson had cried out. But in the next moment, the adults had come to their senses and understood they'd dodged their duty. The adults had righted themselves. They had stood watch, ready to strike, had any enemies attacked.

"They go through the motions of protecting the bud, and they've attempted to deny they're aging," the sobo had said. "But this is futile. The wind has detached the two decayed petals, on each of them. And their other petals are weakened by brown spots. They are experiencing the final stage of withering and weakening. Their strength has faded; they can barely right their stems. They've lost their ability to fight, and their lives flicker, like a burning candle reaching the end of its wick."

Her magomusukos' eyes had turned glassy, and he'd wiped at an escaped tear. "No. We must help them, before all their petals fall to the ground. They aren't *old* yet."

His sobo's downcast eyes had spoken of certain defeat. "We can't. Their time has arrived." The gusty wind had seized the elderly. Their petals had thrashed, and they had attempted to spank the blustery bursts of wind. They had battled to survive, but to no avail. The aging flowers had wobbled from side to side, bumped into each other, and finally, their stems had weakened. Bent over, they'd clung to each other, and they'd tried to hold on. But their perseverance had given way, and their embrace had broken. The screen had shown the wind's impetus had detached the elderly flowers from their stems and sent them into a spiraling motion. And the audio for the wind had changed into the mere whisper of a breeze. But the aging flowers had laid still on the ground. And the mournful instrumental of a single violin had played.

Magomusuko had covered his ears with his hands. "Sobo, I'm finished with this game of pretending."

She'd removed his hands. "I would rather have spared you this lesson, but you must listen and allow me to finish my story. You must understand the cycle. It repeats again and again, with each generation. For cherry blossoms. For humans. The aging flowers wanted to survive. They did their best to hold on. My danna tried his best to stay with me. But like all humans, my husband died. You must understand, Magomusuko, this is the destiny of cherry blossom. This is the fate of all humans, too."

The young boy had tugged at the sleeve of his sobo's kimono. "This ends now. I want to go home."

His grandmother had taken hold of his hand. "Not yet. You must understand human fate, for we share the same destiny as the cherry blossoms. *Death*."

Her magomusuko had wept and shaken with sorrow. She'd kissed his forehead. "I'm sorry. This thorny lesson everyone must learn. But I promise there's a silver lining. Bear with me. I'll finish the story as fast as I can." The flowers had shaken their heads, indicated she would.

The young grandson had shifted his body on the bench, and his eyes had met hers.

"The life of a cherry blossom flower, like a human's life, is brief. Each is beautiful, but each experiences mortality. A cherry blossom sprouts, and we call them a bud. A human is born, and we call them a baby. All humans and the pink cherry blossoms, the Japanese call sakura, grow, live, and die."

The magomusuko had placed his hands over his ears, again. "I don't want to hear anymore," he'd whimpered.

"You must let me finish," she'd said, in a soft voice. She had removed his hands and held them in hers. She'd brought them to her lips, kissed them, and lowered them onto her lap to hold. "I want to tell you about the silver lining, the renewal, or what I prefer to call the rebirth. The next spring brings another season of life. Beauty returns to the tree, with the arrival of new sprouts. And the cycle of life repeats. But it always leads to the inevitable, death. This happens over and over, for every generation."

Her magomusuko had sat up straighter. "Like when a baby is born to replace a human that died?"

"Yes. Like you lightened my grief and replenished my family tree, after my danna died. You are wiser than your years, my beloved grandson."

"So you don't think of him anymore?"

"I will remember and love my danna until death strips me from the family tree. And so it is with all those we have loved, who have vanished: flowers swept away by wicked wind or a downpour of rain, those destroyed by disease, those fallen to their death due to frailty. The sweet scent of their lives lingers in our memory."

Her magomusuko had sniffled. "I wish I could have talked with my grandfather, spent time with him at the park, like I have with you."

"I wish that, too. But have I not shown you pictures of him and told you stories about me and your sofu's years together? Have I not stressed enough his love for family?"

A smile had crept onto his face. "You have, Sobo."

"Through these ways, I've reflected your heritage. For though he died before you emerged from your okaasan's womb, your sofu lingers. I see and sense his presence daily. You have his sympathetic eyes, his caring heart. In you, I see the beautiful flower that left me long ago. Please promise to never forget me."

Her magomusuko had crossed his heart then taken hold of her hand. "Never. I promise."

The remaining cherry blossoms had rejoiced with a dance of thanksgiving for the magomusuko's vow.

A bolt of white lightning had flashed on the backdrop screen. This time, frozen with fright, the remaining cherry blossoms hadn't moved.

The stage lighting had dimmed and focused solely on the grandson and his grandmother. The music had turned gloomy.

"Time for the end of the story. Your sofu calls to me. I must leave you."

The dancers had thrashed their petals, and they'd shook with fear.

"Leave me? You never leave me alone in the park."

The sobo had said, with labored breaths, "It is my time."

"Please. No more pretending."

The music had stopped. His sobo's voice had softened and trembled. "Listen and follow my directions. Get the cell phone from my purse."

The boy's face had tightened with awareness, and he'd done as she'd instructed.

"Call your mother. Tell her to leave work and come to my favorite park bench. She knows which one. Stay by this bench and wait for her. And remember what I've taught you about strangers."

Her magomusuko's eyes had filled with dread. "Sobo!" he'd cried out.

Her eyes had fluttered, like a butterfly's wounded wings. Her head had fallen backward and hung over the back of the park bench. He'd gotten the phone out of her purse and had called. "Mom, hurry. We're at the park. Grandmother's favorite bench. I think she's… she's…" He'd laid the phone on the bench and held his sobo's hand. "You're the best of the cherry blossoms, Sobo." And in a whisper, "I'll see you at the rebirth."

The stage had gone dark. And applause had filled Adelphi Dance Theatre. It had put me on cloud nine. We'd dismounted and lined up shoulder to shoulder behind the curtain. It had reopened, and the lights had gone up and illuminated our cast of dancers. We'd stood downstage during the audiences' standing ovation, and my eyes had scoured the seats. I had located our daughter, Andrea, in the second row. Her passionate smile and enthusiastic clapping had warmed my heart. And coming from my perfectionist daughter, that moment had meant the world to me.

Others in the audience had wiped at their eyes with a tissue. I'd had no doubt the audience had connected with the story we had told through dance: Death is inevitable, but the promise of resurrection is given to those who believe.

The two reporters seated in the front row, who Robert had recruited, had clapped enthusiastically. And the photographer had taken lots of pictures. I'd had no doubt we'd get good reviews, and optimism for drawing additional students had risen up in me. Keeping The Silver Slipper open had developed into a strong possibility.

But Henry Walsh's lawsuit had lingered, like a dark cloud before a thunderstorm. *I'll beg the old fart to drop the charges, if that's what it takes. He'd enjoy seeing me plead. We can't lose the studio. Nadia Slovinskia gifted us with it. She'd roll over in her grave. And if it's taken from us, Alex's heart will break. Mine, too.*

Robert had stood downstage left, on the apron of the stage. After the applause had died down, he'd announced and praised Brandon Lutz as the troupe's production manager, and as an instructor at Adelphi University of Performing Arts. Next, he'd announced himself and Michaela Caplan as dance instructors at Adelphi. And as I had expected, he had praised the university's excellent curriculum.

Plenty of praise for the dance department. Good job, Robert.

"Now, as I announce each troupe member's name, please step forward and take a bow," Robert had said. "Michaela Caplan, the grandmother, and Tyler Partridge, the grandson." Applause had thundered throughout the theatre, and the huge smile on my grandson's face had struck me as priceless. Kami and Brian, as the buds, had taken the second bows. Stephanie and Dave, the teens, had gone third, and Lauren and Matt had stepped forward for the fourth bows.

These members of the dance troupe had stepped back into line. "These last two people own The Silver Slipper dance studio. They've given dance lessons for thirty-four years," Robert had said. "They portrayed the adult cherry blossoms. Would my parents, Alexandra and Ty Partridge, please step forward." We'd taken our bows, and the audience's passionate ovation had gotten me chocked up.

After a second bow call for the troupe members, we had fallen back into line, and Robert had announced the ancillary Adelphi contributors to the performance: The costume design students, the music students, who had provided the CD, and the art students, who had constructed the tree, had moved downstage center and taken their bows. Our son had followed-up with a thank-you to Bruckman Steel, the company that had built the framework for the tree.

The applause had died down. "There's another person I want to acknowledge tonight. Without his help, this performance wouldn't have happened. He's a colleague, a good friend, and an excellent organizer. Please give a big round of applause for Brandon Lutz."

I'd perceived that Robert's last few words would be a thank-you to the audience for attending. But I had needed to say something, and I'd taken the microphone from him. "I can't allow my son to leave this stage before I thank him for his endless efforts." A lump of fatherly love had formed in my throat. I'd taken a deep breath before I had continued. "All of us in the dance troupe appreciate your attendance and your applause tonight. Thank-you. But before you leave, I'd like to acknowledge mine and Alex's son. Robert put the choreography together, he reached out to talented Adelphi staff and students to enlist help, and he battled one obstacle after another to make tonight a reality. Please join me in a round of applause for Robert Partridge."

At my request he'd taken a bow, and the audience's appreciation had sounded throughout the theatre. And a thought had entered my mind, *I'll remember this night forever. Thank-you, Son.*

Chapter 35 - The Clouds
Saturday July 29

Robert, Brandon, and the other members of the dance troupe had lingered to savor the success of the performance, but Alex and I had made our way to the east side exit, where Andrea had said she'd meet us.

"No," a loud, masculine voice had said. Both of us had turned and looked down the hallway. The man had tugged at the black briefcase the woman held. "Sis, let me carry that for you."

"It's that gaudily dressed woman and the guy with the long hair we saw earlier," Alex had said.

The woman had pulled the case free from his grasp, and she'd shouted a string of profanities as she'd headed toward the exit. The man had followed her out of the Performing Arts Center.

"Mouthy old gal," Alex had said. "You think they attended our performance?"

"I guess. Sure glad she didn't get loud in the theatre."

Alex and I had met up with Andrea. "Congratulations," she'd said. "I loved the performance, Mom and Dad."

"Thank-you, Andrea," Alex had said.

I'd given our daughter a kiss on the cheek. "Yeah, thanks, Sweetheart."

"I'll give Robert a call tomorrow and congratulate him, too. I think he'll be busy celebrating tonight."

We'd exited Adelphi Performing Arts Center, and the three of us had begun our walk toward the parking garage. Darkness, like a veil, had distorted our surroundings. And for some reason, perhaps to confirm that our performance had taken place, I'd turned around, looked back. Light had glowed through the elongated, vertical windows of the red brick building. And a silent prayer had run through my mind,

God, please help our newspaper reviews and word of mouth draw students to The Silver Slipper.

A loud crack of thunder had sounded. "We'd better get moving," I'd coaxed Alex and Andrea along. LED pole lights had guided our way, but the wind had swished through the bare tree branches, and sharp, popping noises had sounded, as if small, brittle twigs had succumbed to the wind's force and snapped. "Those dark clouds look like they're ready to dump buckets of rain," I'd said. "We'd better move faster."

Thunder had grumbled, like a constipated old man who couldn't purge, and clouds the color of slate had spread across the sky. And an unusual shaped one with varied gray shadings had tantalized my curiosity.

Drops of rain had pinged the top of my bald head, and I had hurried my wife and daughter along. Our steps had turned into a jog, but the configuration of that one cloud had continued to tease my imagination. *It reminds me of something. But what?* We'd kept up our hurried pace, but the cloud's shape had imprinted in my brain and held my interest. *Long hair trailing out? Yeah, like the wind's caught it*, I'd thought. *And I see an eye, and a nose. The cloud looks like the silhouette of a woman's face.*

The rain had slowed, turned to drizzle. I had turned and pointed behind us. "Look at the shape of that cloud. What does it remind you of?"

Alex had laughed, "One trip to SoHo to buy a painting and your dad's finding art in the sky."

Andrea had laughed, something I hadn't heard her do for a while. Thankful for her one night of relief from the George Washington Bridge Case, my attention to the cloud's configuration had diminished. I had taken hold of Alex's hand, and the three of us had continued to our destination, Andrea's car.

"Mom and Dad, I'm so proud of you. Your performances tonight made you standouts on that stage," Andrea had said. "Working on this high-profile case has distracted me. I'm sorry. I should have shown more interest in your work. In my brother's, too."

"Your mother and I understand. You're under a lot of stress."

Andrea had sighed. "Yes, but I can handle it. So stop worrying."

A shiny coating of tears had formed on Alex's eyes. "Thank-you for attending tonight; it meant the world to us."

"Yeah, Sweetheart, thanks for coming. And know that your mom and I are proud of you for wanting to get justice for the deceased victim's family. But please be careful."

"Don't worry. I am."

Growing close to our destination, the parking garage near the Motamed Athletic Field, white bolts of lightning had sliced through the sky's gray backdrop, and claps of thunder had followed. Alex's body had shuddered in response to the storm's acoustics, and I had tightened my grip on her hand. The wind's force had grown fierce and had pushed us from behind. Andrea had staggered, and I'd told her to take hold of my other arm. An immediate downpour had followed, and the rain had struck us with sideways blows. What should have amounted to a short walk to the garage had turned into a head-on, grueling battle with a wicked thunderstorm.

Andrea's free hand had secured one side of her hair and doing so had allowed her to see the walking path. My wife had attempted to do the same, but her long hair had blown forward and covered her face. With locked arms, we'd leaned into the whipping wind. But this surge of rain and wind hadn't let up. My glasses had flooded, creating a wavy distortion of reality, and I'd stopped to take them off. I'd shoved them in my pocket.

Our daughter had announced, "I see the parking garage."

Alex's arm, interlocked with mine, had shaken. "You're chilled to the bone," I'd said.

"Dad, my car has a great heater. It'll warm Mom up in no time."

Andrea had stopped by one of the LED pole lights, freed her interlocked arm from mine. "You and Mom get inside. I need this light to find my keys." She had dug through the contents in her purse.

"We'll wait with you."

"No. It's pouring. Get Mom out of the rain."

Alex and I had entered the garage and stood next to our daughter's car. We'd heard her scream, followed by a shriek of, "Don't, please!"

"Ty," my wife had gasped. "Someone's hurting her!"

Can't leave Alex by herself. I had grabbed her hand, and we'd taken off running the direction I'd thought Andrea's scream had come from. Winded, we'd stopped.

Alex had clamped her free hand over her mouth. Her body had shaken in sync with her broken sobs. "We're not going to find her," she'd cried out.

"I'm going to call 911. Stay close to me." The heavy, steady downpour had buzzed, like a swarm of bees. Coupled with booms of thunder and shrill gusts of wind, my cell's transmission had failed the first time. But I'd gotten through on the second try.

"They'll be here in minutes," I had reassured Alex and taken hold of her trembling hand again. "I gave them a description of Andrea and told them she's in a blue dress."

In vain, we'd turned, looked in every direction, and listened for movement or further vocal sounds. But the merciless rain had pinged on the sidewalk, and the thunder had rumbled. The wind's furious whistle had raked through the skeletal tree branches, and a sorrowful howl, like weeping, had sounded. Masked by nature's temper tantrum, our hearing and sight hadn't given us any further clues to our daughter's whereabouts. "The university grounds might as well be a maze," Alex's words had wobbled with emotion. "We aren't going to find her, Ty. What if a rapist has her?"

"She's a fighter," I'd said, though her uncharacteristic pleading earlier had sent a chill up my spine. *I bet he had his hand over her mouth, and she bit him to cry out for help*, my thoughts had reassured me. *But now he has her moving again. What direction? Please. Bite him. Do whatever you can. But cry out again, Andrea.*

Another slice of lightning had cut through the dark sky, and its partner, a thunderous clap, had sounded. The whipping, whooshing sounds from tree branches had grown louder. *If Andrea does cry out again, we might not hear her.* And another agonizing thought had occurred. *What if she can't?* "We'll find her, Honey," I'd said. But in truth I'd needed assurance myself. "The police will be here any–" A catch had formed in my throat, and Alex had taken hold of my hand. Rivulets of tears had run down her cheeks. And I'd pulled myself together.

What if he watched Alex and I exit the garage? Did he double back with Andrea to get her car? I had taken Alex by the hand, and we'd run back to the garage. The car hadn't been taken. "She tossed her keys. She's too smart for this guy, Honey." *Who has her? And why?* Possible assailants had flashed through my mind. *A random pervert? Someone Commissioner Fulcono hired? Or he, himself?*

Another bolt of white lightning had shot through the sky. As if it had illuminated my brain's memory, a face had come into view. *Dr.*

Henry Walsh attended the performance. Can't prove he butchered Andrea and Tom's Pomeranian, but he has surgical instruments. And he's for sure a nutcase. A pervert, too. And he hates my guts for kicking him out of class. He wants to ruin Alex and me financially. But he's not stupid; he knows he won't win the lawsuit. I told him Maria and the other women in class will testify. Andrea fight. He's old. But what if he sedated her? God, please don't let him kill her.

Or is this Commissioner Giovanni Fulcono's scare tactic to get Andrea to throw the case? Was he in the audience tonight? I'd concentrated, scanning my memory. *I didn't see him, but that doesn't mean he wasn't there.*

At his office, he'd said he'd do anything to save his son, Michael, from prison. Kidnapping? Murder? Then it had struck me that something else was at stake, too. *If the jury convicts Michael Fulcono, the Commissioner will take a political hit. He might get forced to retire as Transit Commissioner.*

My thoughts had shattered, like broken glass. "I hear footsteps," I'd whispered to Alex.

"Me, too. Police?"

"Maybe. But walk behind me."

We'd continued combing Adelphi's grounds, as quietly as we could. The caller's message at the studio had crept into my mind.

"Alex," I'd whispered, "let's stop and listen." We'd stood still and hoped to break through the barrier of the thunderstorm's tantrum, hoped to hear movement, or better yet, voices. The minutes had ticked away, and we'd had no clue of Andrea's whereabouts. And my mind had darkened with morbid what-ifs. *Either her attacker had a getaway car and he's left Adelphi Campus with her, or her dead body is lying on the rain-soaked ground.* A sickening taste had snaked its way up my throat.

My optimism to find our daughter had dwindled, and I'd decided to call out. "Andrea! Andrea!" I had prayed she could hear me. And I'd hoped she could answer.

"Someone's after us," Alex had said.

We'd stopped, turned around, listened. I'd taken her hand and whispered, "Stay close to me." The sound of feet splashing through puddles had broken through the rain's intensity and grown faster, louder. "I don't know who's closing in on us, Honey. But it's more than one person." I'd sucked in gulps of air, and I had attempted to catch my breath. I had let go of Alex's hand. "Get behind me."

White lights had blinded us. I'd stood in front of Alex, my fists balled up, ready to fight.

"Police. Put your hands up!"

We had complied. "I'm the one who called," I'd said. "Someone kidnapped our daughter, Andrea Warden. We're Ty and Alex Partridge."

"You," one of the officers had pointed at me, "reach in your pocket with your left hand, get your driver's license, and hand it to me." Two other officers had kept their guns aimed at us.

In slow-motion I'd gotten my wallet out and handed it to the officer, who'd given the impression he'd been in charge. He had shined his flashlight on my license, then told the other officers to holster their guns.

"I'm Officer Ryan with the Garden City Police Department. We have an all-points-bulletin out for your daughter. Officers are scouring the campus for her now, Mr. and Mrs. Partridge. If the perpetrator has remained on the premises with her, we'll find them. Brookland Police have a description of your daughter, too, and they've set up surveillance on the bridges. We think the kidnapper's means of escape is by car, so all exits leading to the bridges and expressways are being covered. The police are authorized to stop any male with a female occupant, or any male by himself. The perp would likely have Andrea restrained and in the trunk of his car."

Tears had welled up in my wife's eyes.

"I'm sorry," Officer Ryan had said. "I understand you're upset, but please bear with me. You gave us a description, but if we had a picture of her that would be better."

Alex had opened her purse, rummaged through pictures in her wallet. "Here," she'd said and handed one to him. "It's from a couple of years ago. Her hair's shorter now, but other than that she looks the same."

"Good," Officer Ryan had said. "This'll help. We'll get an APB out to the stations in the surrounding counties, with Andrea's picture. Do either of you have any idea who might have kidnapped Andrea and why?"

"Yes," I'd said. "I think it's one of two men."

The officer pulled a small note pad from inside his vest.

"Henry Walsh. I believe he could have done this for revenge."

"W-a-l-s-h?"

"Yes," I had said.

"Revenge for what?"

"I kicked him out of dance class."

The officer's forehead had wrinkled, and he'd hesitated, as if he'd had to let this bit of information soak in. "I find it difficult to believe someone would go to such an extreme over dance lessons."

"Henry's a dirty old man. He got vulgar with the ladies in dance class."

"I see. By old, what age do you mean, Mr. Partridge?"

"At least eighty."

The officer had paused from taking notes. "Who is the other man?"

"Commissioner Giovanni Fulcono."

The officer's right eyebrow had arched, and his eyes had held steady on me. Seconds of awkward silence had hung between us before his eyebrow relaxed. "Why would *he* take your daughter, Mr. Partridge?"

"She's the prosecutor for the George Washington Bridge Case. His son, Michael is on trial for vehicular manslaughter."

Officer Ryan had taken a deep breath, and this time both of his eyebrows had arched. He'd stared at me and remained silent.

My wife's face had turned red, and she'd frowned. I'd thought she was going to give Officer Ryan a piece of her mind. Instead, a flood of tears had rolled down her cheeks. "Our daughter has gotten death threats!"

He had made eye contact with Alex. "I'm sorry. I understand you're scared. But I've known Commissioner Fulcono for more than a decade. He's a good man, but his son–"

Officer Ryan has an opinion about Michael, but he's apprehensive about sharing it.

"Give me your cell number, Mr. Partridge, and I'll keep you up-to-date on whatever leads we get. But you need to let us take charge of the search for Andrea. We don't need you or your wife taken hostage or killed. Go home."

I had nodded, as if I'd agreed, but no way was I going home, no way could I convince Alex to go. Her sideways, defiant glare at Officer Ryan's advice had spoken clear as words. *Dear God, help us find Andrea alive and unharmed*, I'd thought.

The officers had dispersed to continue their search. And Alex's teary eyes had met mine. "We can't give up, Ty."

"We're not. But stay behind me."

Alex and I had forged ahead. The rain's tempo had slowed, and its ping as it had hit the leaves had softened. At intervals I'd stopped, turned around, and made sure my wife had remained close.

Movement from behind us had drawn our attention. We had turned around and looked back. There had stood the gaudily dressed, artsy looking woman, who Alex and I had seen in the PAC hallway, arguing with a man. She had had her left arm locked around Andrea's throat, and the shiny blade of a knife pressed against our daughter's carotid artery. "Stand in front of your daughter," she'd ordered Alex.

"Stay where you are, Honey," I'd said.

In one, swift movement, the woman had moved the blade up and across our daughter's forehead, and blood had trickled out. Just as quick, she had returned the blade to Andrea's carotid artery. "Follow my orders, Mama, or I'll slit little Mrs. Lawyer's throat." The woman's large, triangular earrings had swung back and forth and glistened in the dark. Her frenzied eyes had glared at me as the corners of her lips turned up. In the next second, her shrill, malicious laugh, like that of a mad person, screeched through the silence, and I'd assumed the police had to have heard it.

"Don't do it, Alex," I'd said. But she had stepped in front of our daughter, had become Andrea's shield.

She's crazy. And she intends to kill them both. Then my brain had registered the full extent of what the woman had said. *Mrs. Lawyer's throat. She's Fulcono's wife?*

An image of the tapered piece of broken plate in our kitchen and the family photos had flashed through my mind. *The omens.*

The woman had pressed the shimmering blade taut against the front of Andrea's neck. "How do you like that, Mrs. High and Mighty?" Alex had gasped. The mix of my wife's tears and the hopelessness in her eyes had fueled me with a course of action.

Knock the old nutcase down, my inner voice had spoken. *No*, common sense had countered. *She'll slit Andrea's throat with one swift slash and have time to slit Alex's, too.*

"Take me," I had shouted. "Let my wife and daughter go. Kill me instead."

"Shut up you fool. The lawyer's the only one I wanted, but you two got in the way. I threatened her. I killed her little mutt! But she wouldn't throw the case. I'd say she's a slow learner."

Alex had shot me a pleading glance, and as she'd shifted her big, warm, brown eyes toward our daughter, a tear had rolled down her cheek. And I'd understood. She's begging me to save Andrea.

"Mrs. Fulcono, please," I'd said.

"Don't you dare call me that! Susan and my dear brother, Giovanni, are thieves! Michael is *my* son, and he isn't going to prison. Are you on board, now, Partridge?" She had let loose with a malicious laugh, and her silver earrings had swung at a frenzied tempo.

She said Partridge. Her voice. I've heard it before. Where? How do I bargain with this mad person? As I'd studied the woman who'd held my wife and daughter hostage, she'd grown more animated and bobbled her head. Her large, triangular earrings had swung in furious motion again. *Those earrings. I've seen them before. Where? Heard her gruff, irritating voice somewhere else, too. Angela's baby shower.* "Mrs. Schrader?"

"Well, good for you. You've put it together, Mr. Partridge. Michael Fulcono was born Michael Schrader." The slight turn of her head had indicated she'd heard feet sloshing through the wet grass, like I had, like my wife's sideways glance had indicated that she had, too.

"The police." Mrs. Schrader had drawn out the S sound, as if she'd hissed. "I'm going to catch you up and kill your daughter and wife before they find us.

"Less than a month after I had given birth to Michael, my husband had a heart attack and died. I suffered from depression, and my so-called brother and sister-in-law had me declared unfit to raise my son. They put me in a facility for the mentally ill. Medicine, shock treatments, and no visits from Giovanni and Susan. But the worst of it was separation from my baby.

"I got released from that hellhole after Michael's second birthday. I begged Giovanni and Susan to let me see him. They allowed it with the stipulation I had to pretend I was Aunt Miranda. They demanded I let them adopt my son, or they'd take me to court. Given my diagnosis and stay at the mental facility, they'd convinced me they would win.

"My handsome little boy didn't have any reason to want to leave the only parents he'd known. Giovanni and Susan had filled their home with toys, books, and a puppy, and Michael had two loving parents. If I had removed him from all of that, my son would have hated me.   "Robbed of motherhood, I touched the fringes of Michael's life. Aunt Miranda only visited on holidays and brought her nephew gifts. And though I've single-handedly built a successful graphic design company, how can you or anyone else think that lessens the hurt of not raising my son?"

The lightning had surrendered. The rain, nothing more than a drizzle, had no longer camouflaged the woman's raucous voice. *The police will hear her, close in, and overtake her. Play to her arrogance. Bow to her sense of superiority and buy time.* "You're right, Mrs. Schrader. Angela has complimented your business savvy. Few men could develop a company as lucrative as you have."

She'd lifted her chin and her lips had turned upward into a prideful smile.

The sound of feet splashing through puddles had grown louder. Mrs. Schrader must have heard it, too. She had broken eye contact with me, and in a quick, jerky motion she'd turned her neck to listen. But just as quick, she had returned her attention to me. And I hadn't had time to attack and take the knife from her. I had looked down at the ground, feigned submission.

I'd guessed about twenty minutes had passed since Andrea, Alex, and I had walked out of the Performing Arts Center. Silence hung between the four of us, and the point of Mrs. Schrader's knife had remained poised to take Andrea's life. I had reassured myself. *The police are close by. Stall.*

Alex had decided to play to Mrs. Schrader's narcissism, too. "Angela told us your company is the best in New York City. She–"

A man's voice had interrupted. "Don't do it, Miranda," he'd said and approached Mrs. Schrader. *He's the man we saw with Mrs. Schrader in the PAC's hallway,* I'd thought. He had removed his glasses and the mop of long graying hair with his left hand. And he'd let them fall to the ground.

"It's over Miranda. Give me the knife."

"Commissioner Fulcono!"

"Yes. It's me, Mr. Partridge. My sister's sick. Let me take care of this. Miranda–"

"Shut up, you thief," she'd said, her voice saturated with malice. "Don't interfere, or I'll cut your throat, too." The thin stream of red had continued to run down Andrea's neck. "Neither of you can stop me. Lawyer Warden isn't putting *my* son in prison."

One of the police officers Alex and I had talked to before had shown up and shined a flashlight in Schrader's eyes. The other two had had their firearms drawn and pointed at her.

Thank-you, God, had shot through my mind.

"Let's talk lady," the officer holding the flashlight had said.

Mrs. Schrader hadn't flinched. "Get that light out of my eyes." She had maintained her grip on my daughter's left arm and kept the knife's point teased to Andrea's neck. In one swift, upward movement, her right hand had made a diagonal sweep, and the knife's blade had glistened. She'd cut the brown beauty mark off above Andrea's left eyebrow. Blood had gushed and run down her cheek.

I had lunged at Mrs. Schrader, as had two of the officers, but in a quick stroke she had returned the blade to our daughter's neck. "Step back. All of you. I'm in charge."

Blood had continued running down the side of Andrea's neck in a wavy line, and her low sobs had borne a hole into me. *The cloud shaped like a woman's profile predicted my daughter's fate.*

"Put away your guns, or I'll kill them both," Mrs. Schrader had shouted at the police officers.

The officer who'd acted as if he had been in charge told the other officers to holster their guns. As they'd complied, I had inched a step closer to Mrs. Schrader.

"That's right. Move closer Partridge. Then your wife's and daughter's deaths are on you. Stand in front of me Mom. Move!"

Tears had run down Andrea's cheeks, and she'd shook from silenced sobs. "Don't kill my mother. Please. She has nothing to do with your son's trial."

The love of my life is the crazy woman's shield. God, help me choose the right thing to do.

Schrader's face had beamed with a self-assured smirk. "Now for the grand finale, Lawyer Warden, Partridge family."

The police had stood their ground, weapons holstered. *If they rush the crazy, old bat, she'll kill Andrea and Alex.*

The same officer, the one who had acted like he was in charge, had said, "Drop the knife, lady. You don't want to spend the rest of your life in prison."

Mrs. Schrader had responded with a show of arrogance. She'd lifted her chin in defiance. "Prison? That supposed to scare me? Send me to hell if you want. I have nothing to lose. What I value is long gone, raising Michael, years of love I'd have given and received. Go ahead. Kill me. I'll take these women with me."

"There's a way out of this," I'd said and inched closer. "Take me. The parking garage is close. You can get away, then kill me if you must have revenge."

"Miranda, you're sick. Let me take you to a doctor," Giovanni Fulcono had said.

Mrs. Schrader's eyes had burned with hate. "Giovanni, I slept, ate, existed in that loony place you dumped me in. I listened to a psychiatrist babble about my inability to handle life's blows. How my lack of coping skills had made me crazy. But I wasn't when you and Susan had me admitted. Maybe I am now. If I am, it's your fault and your infertile wife's fault!"

"I feel for you, lady. You've had a rough go of it," Officer Ryan had said. Mrs. Schrader had focused her attention on him.

Smart move. Keep her attention. Feed her more sympathy. I had inched closer to her while the officer had continued to play his role, like that of a doting son. I'd gotten within a step of Mrs. Schrader, my wife, my daughter. But, as if the woman's crazed mind had reorganized to deal with unfinished business, her attention had returned to her brother. She'd lunged at Giovanni Fulcono and driven the knife into his chest. His body had folded up like an accordion. Alex had seized the opportunity and pushed Andrea out of harm's way. But Mrs. Schrader's reflexes, quick as a cat, had extracted the crimson blade, and her hand sliced through the air with it in a wide arc. I had grabbed for her arm to overpower her, but Alex, having the same idea, had gotten in the way. Shots had fired.

Chapter 36 - Guilt and Closure

Is it morning yet? I had searched for my glasses on the nightstand. Armed with sight, I'd reached for the lamp and turned it on. The face of the alarm clock had illuminated my harsh reality, loneliness. And I had watched the minute hand tick away three minutes. I'd blinked and made a wish. But my inner voice had whispered, *Can't erase it.*

Six weeks had passed. I had tried to imagine how Giovanni Fulcono's wife would recover. She'd viewed the aftermath, but she hadn't observed the killing. She hadn't watched his life slip away. She hadn't heard the gurgling sounds of her husband's final breaths.

Mrs. Schrader had lived, but who'd have missed her if she hadn't? Not Susan Fulcono, the grieving wife. Not the crazy woman's biological son. How could Michael forgive the woman he called Aunt Miranda? How?

What I'd had to reckon with the rest of my life had possessed me. Coldness had numbed me, though the second week of September the temperature had remained warmed. I'd heard the officers' pistols fire and watched both of my dark-haired beauties fall to the ground. One had laid curled up on her side, and her long hair had draped her profile like a curtain. The other had laid face down. Had I attended to the wrong one first? Would they both have lived if I'd chosen differently? Questions had echoed over and over. And my mind had continued playing that night back.

Tears had flowed from my eyes. Guilt, my tormentor, had stabbed at my heart. I hadn't understood what the canvas had depicted. I hadn't imagined our performance, *Dance of Cherry Blossoms,* would lead to my wife's death.

The painting with two women waiting at the shoreline with outstretched arms and the man rowing against the storm's might had confused me the day Alex had bought the picture. I'd studied it in our living room, but I hadn't decided *who'd* needed rescuing. Had I understood its message, nothing bad would have happened. I'd have stopped it.

Self-hate had chewed another piece of my heart away. Confused by the artist's meaning, unaware of his story, I had failed to protect my loved ones. My comprehension had arrived too late. I hadn't understood this omen.

The wind's force had masked the two dark haired women's faces. One's long strands had streamed out in front and had wrapped like fingers, and it had blocked her features. And the other's shorter locks had swept forward with the artist's jagged brushstrokes. How could I tell their ages? The artist had left me no clue. Two sisters caught off-guard by a storm?
 Or two friends?

I hadn't understood the rower's incentive to save the women, either. He hadn't acted as a random man, a Good Samaritan. He'd acted out of devotion to his loved ones. The picture had predicted my attempt to save my wife and daughter.

The cloud had presented itself as we had walked toward the parking garage. It had resembled a woman's facial profile. And the blemish at the tail of her eyebrow, why hadn't I connected that brown dot? Andrea had had her beauty mark since childhood.

But then, I hadn't grasped what the other omens had indicated, either. The tapping across my back, family pictures on the wall. If only I'd understood. The red whipped cream running down my pancakes in rivulets. The bladelike piece of plate. I hadn't deciphered any of the omens.

Grief had laid heavy on my chest, and I'd shut the world out. In the silence, my pulse had beat in my left ear, like a drumroll. And the door to my memory had unlocked. I'd recollected the first time I met Alex Carbone, or Alexandra, as Nadia Slovinskia had called her dance instructor. Young and with no money, I had approached Nadia, the owner of The Silver Slipper. I'd asked her for a dance instructor's job. She'd had me audition with Alex. Taken with the girl's long, dark hair, slender body, and her sexy smile, I had had a tough time focusing on leading her.

Another memory had tugged at my heart, May nineteenth of 1972. A lanky, twenty-two-year-old had presented a black velvet ring box to the love of his life. *My beautiful, kind Alex.* Her answer of, "Yes," had echoed in my head, brought both tears of joy and sorrow.

My mind's eye had jumped to June ninth of 1973. The sun had shined through the stained-glass windows in Saint Michael's Church, and the illusion of colored jewels had glittered on Alex's wedding dress. She'd looked like an angel.

Our first-born, Robert, and the memory of holding him in my arms for the first time had come into view. *Thank-you, Alex.*

The births of our beautiful twin girls had revisited me, too. My heart had flooded with more joy. But my bottom lip had trembled, too, and I'd wondered who Andrea and Angela would confide in when they had problems. And our grandkids hadn't spoken of their nana without crying. I had burned the painting, watched it turn to ash. But the nightmare had continued to visit me. Again, I'd awaken in a cold sweat.

Restless, I had gotten up, gone to the window and parted the mauve drapes. The sun had kissed the horizon, and blurred shapes had come into view. *God's impressionistic art of nature*, I'd thought. A mist had begun to rise up from the center of the street, and an odd thing had happened. Though the window had remained closed, the scent of cherry blossoms had swum up my nose. The strange vapor had begun to spin, and it had revolved faster and faster, teasing my imagination. I had wished for more light. And God had granted my wish. The sun had touched the horizon and showcased the silhouette of an elongated spinning shape.

I'm hallucinating, I'd thought. *My yearning has triggered my imagination.* I'd pressed my face to the glass, and the warmth on my skin had verified the opposite. With my eyes held steady, I had attempted to identify the whirling object.

Dawn had brought clarity. The mist had faded away and exposed the figure of a woman. My heart had hammered against my chest. *Am I losing my mind? No. I'm familiar with every inch of this woman's body. It belongs to my beautiful Alex.*

As I had watched her pirouetting with the gracefulness of a professional ballerina, I'd pounded on the glass to draw her attention. She'd stopped spinning, turned and smiled that special way that had always made me lose my train of thought.

I'd heard a voice inside my head, one I'd known well. "Bird," my sister, Allison, had said, "God has granted you this moment."

Lightheaded, I had gulped and sucked in a mouthful of air. My knees had threatened to buckle. I had tried to digest the sight of my wife. "Allison, help me. This is all too much to handle."

"Steady yourself, Bird," my sister had said. "That night Reverend Maynard and I visited you, I meant to prepare you for what was going to happen. But the reverend put me in my place, cut my words short. Now I can tell you what I wanted to say that night. Sometimes God uses one person to help another. He used my Hannah as an instrument to steady your faith. One minute you believed in God, but in the next your faith waivered, and you were a doubting Thomas, like when the reverend's spirit visited you. And when I spoke to you through him. Bird, you doubted God's work and wrote it off as a dream. But believe me, everything that happened during my daughter's hospitalization, God orchestrated. Chance had nothing to do with you meeting P. J. in Wakefield Memorial's chapel, either. God made it serve as part of His plan to secure your faith, to ensure your rebirth."

"But if you had told me, I could have prevented Alex's death."

"No, the life God meant to save was Andrea's, and she lives."

A sour taste had inched up my throat, and I had thought I'd vomit. "I didn't act quick enough. I wanted to be the martyr; the sacrifice was mine to make . . . not hers."

"God ordained everything that happened, Bird. It's why Alex chose the painting with two women on shore. And He planted the idea for *Dance of Cherry Blossoms* in your head."

"I burned the painting, Allison!" I had attempted to catch my breath. But my chest had grown heavy, burdened with weight.

"Alex was the woman in front, the one meant to protect her daughter from the storm," Allison had said. "The man in the boat was you."

"I wish I had died instead. Her kindness and beautiful smile turned me into putty. What I'd give to hold her in my arms, run my hands through her long, dark hair, and kiss her. I'll love her forever.

"When The Silver Slipper's enrollment declined, I agreed to take Robert's help to save it, Allison. Tom told me about the threatening calls Andrea had received. And when Spanky's bloodied body was discovered, I should have backed away from the performance. What if Mrs. Schrader had had a gun in the theatre? I gave that crazy woman the opportunity to get to my family. I'm responsible for my wife's death," I'd said.

A crushing pain had radiated across my chest, and the bedroom had filled with the scent of cherry blossoms. I'd doubled over in pain, and Alex had appeared before me as beautiful as she'd looked in life.

She'd wrapped her arms around me, and with no words she'd shown me the intensity of her love.

As if her voice had transported from a faraway place, she'd said, "Your pain will cease in a few seconds, like mine did. And you'll experience your rebirth. Heaven awaits you, and it's grander than you can imagine."

The scent of cherry blossoms had surrounded me, like a comfortable blanket. With jagged breaths, I'd managed to say, "Alex, I pledge my vow of everlasting love to you."

"And I to you, as we share eternity." Her lips had caressed mine, and I had held onto her for support. Hazy shapes had begun to materialize of people I'd once known, who'd fallen from the tree of life. And the spirits had formed a circle around Alex and me. My sister, Allison, had smiled in the sweet, shy way she had when we'd been kids. She'd cuddled my stillborn nephew, Jacob, who'd died in 1972. Unscathed by the throes of death, he had giggled and kicked his feet, healthy and alert. Reverend Maynard's blue eyes had twinkled, and he'd nodded at me. And Pop Bradshaw, my former dance instructor in Greenstone, Missouri, had grinned at me. No longer hunched over he'd cut a rug with a woman, as if keeping time to swing dance music. "I bet that's his wife Mary," I'd said to Alex. And the former owner of The Silver Slipper, Nadia Slovinskia, had moved fluently toward me and Alex. She had no trace of arthritis, like she'd had in her human form. Along with her, our children's other adopted grandmother, Margaret, had approached us. And both greeted us with warm embraces. I had observed an elderly lady smiling at me. *Who is she?* I'd thought. And God had spoken to me, like He had in Wakefield Memorial's Chapel. "Your prayer initiated my work. And through the hospital chaplain the Holy Spirit entered Helen's heart and saved her soul from damnation. Meet P. J.'s wife, who embraced Christianity on her deathbed. Good work, Ty Partridge."

The pleasant smell of cherry blossoms had grown stronger, filled my lungs. And a sense of harmony with the spirits who had surrounded me had added a dimension of happiness I had not experienced in my former life.

"Alex, my love, together we'll await the arrival of our human loved ones." I had taken her in my arms and had held her close. Waltz music had begun to play, and in my reborn state, I'd said, "May I have this dance, lovely lady?"

"You may." Alex had smiled that special way, and as if my heart had still ticked, I'd have sworn it raced.

Also by Audrey Murphy

Bird's Flight

Read the prequel to *Rebirth*, *Bird's Flight*. Bird escapes his fate of small town coal miner and moves to New York where he finds dancing, love, and the power to pursue his dreams against all odds. Known as Bird to family and friends, Ty Partridge is destined for the fate of all young men in his rural Missouri town. He, too, will surely end up working in the coal mines. Bird befriends Pop- the elderly owner of the local soda fountain shop-and Pop soon realizes Bird has much higher hopes for himself. Bird's passion is for dance. In order to escape Greenstone, Bird has to go against his family and the town traditions. With Pop's help, he quickly becomes an outsider as he makes his way to New York City to pursue his dream of being a performer. Bird's new reality is a little too real though, as he comes up against crime and the threat of ending up homeless. He soon makes the acquaintance of Nadia Slovinskia, who introduces Bird to her employee, Alexandra, the most beautiful woman Ty has ever seen. With the help of these women and his new city, Ty learns the importance of willpower and perseverance when pursuing his dreams, but he also must ask himself: are all dreams worth pursuing?

About the Author

Audrey Murphy, a former teacher, lives in Maryville, Illinois, with her husband. She has two adult sons. She is an avid reader and enjoys dancing.